The Cartographer of Lost Winds

A Novel

Hichem Karoui

Global East-West (London)

Contents

For my beloved sisters — Latifa, Lilia, Faten, and Awatef —
The first cartographers of my heart.
And for the people of Tunis, with whom I shared years that shaped my heart and memory.
To the city whose streets, scents, and silences breathe like a living soul.

The city, however, does not tell its past, but contains it like the lines of a hand, written in the corners of the streets, the gratings of the windows, the banisters of the steps, the antennae of the lightning rods, the poles of the flags, every segment marked in turn with scratches, indentations, scrolls.

— **Italo Calvino, *Invisible Cities***

A man sets out to draw the world. As the years go by, he peoples a space with images of provinces, kingdoms, mountains, bays, ships, islands, fishes, rooms, instruments, stars, horses, and individuals. A short time before he dies, he discovers that that patient labyrinth of lines traces the image of his own face.

— **Jorge Luis Borges, *The Maker***

1
Whispers of the Past

Tunis. Late 1970s

Karim Mansour sank deeper into the tattered pages of Sufi poetry spread across his small wooden table. Each line resonated with an elegance he could not participate in socially, yet he felt a profound connection to the emotions embedded within the words. The delicate dance of language offered him solace, an escape from his own reality, where attempts at human connection often resulted in a stilted silence. The Sufi poetry, with its profound insights into the human condition, became his refuge, a source of comfort and understanding in his solitary life. As the ink flowed under his fingertips, he felt like a silent translator, an interpreter of souls but never quite one himself.

His translations were meticulous, capturing the essence of mysticism and longing that filled the texts, revealing layers he feared to express in the flesh.

Late at night, as the moon cast ghostly shadows through his window, illuminating the manuscripts before him, he found himself entwined in the echoes of their sentiments. The verses dripped with a poignant melancholy: a reminder of the warmth of shared humanity, a warmth he clumsily skirted, fearful of the vulnerability that came with genuine connection.

Even as his lips moved to utter the rhymes silently, his heart ached with the realisation that these lines spoke of love and belonging. Concepts he kept behind closed doors. Each stanza felt like a thread tugging at the edges of his solitude, whispering promises of intimacy he instinctively recoiled from. To translate was to control an intangible essence; to communicate was to relinquish that control, and therein lay the chasm he dared not cross, a chasm filled with the fear of vulnerability.

Yet, tonight felt different. As his pen skated across the parchment, he found his mind drifting to a deeply buried memory. A fleeting encounter with kindness from years past that now beckoned him. The laughter of distant friends reverberated in his consciousness, mingling with the poetry that flowed through his veins. Perhaps he could draw upon these remnants, allow them to spill onto his pages and breathe life back into his desolate heart.

But as the moon dipped toward its zenith, a sound intruded upon his reverie—a whisper maddeningly familiar, weaving through the stillness of his flat. He raised his head, listening intently, the sanctity of his solitude shattered by an echo of a voice he thought long forgotten. The words drifted in and out of his consciousness like a tide, impossible to grasp yet impossible to ignore. Who was it that called to him from the corridors of memory, daring him to unveil the obscured connections of his solitary life, and step into the potential for connection that lay beyond?

Compelled by a mix of curiosity and fear, he placed his translations aside, the scent of aged paper mingling with the faint tang of jasmine wafting through his open window. Those delicate whispers spoke not just of past transgressions, but of paths he had forsaken. The threads connecting him to the world outside those four familiar walls. The poetry lay still before him, yet a burgeoning need to explore beyond the confines of translation surged within him, a need that tugged at his comfort zones. What awaited him outside in the labyrinthine Medina if he dared to step into the unknown?

As he ventured into the night, the weight of his unfinished translations pressed against his heart, and the profound silence of his flat became a distant memory. Each step he took echoed back promises of lost connections and unfulfilled yearnings, hinting that perhaps his silence was not his only companion. The gentle embrace of the evening air hinted that destiny itself was stitched into the very fabric of the night, urging him forward toward what he had long evaded: connection.

Little did he know that the path before him would lead him deeper into the labyrinth, and there, the whispers of the past would become entangled with the currents of fate he had yet to understand, a fate woven from the threads of his memories and present choices.

***

The verses danced on the aged pages like spectres conjured from forgotten dreams. Karim leaned closer to the words, allowing the cadences of the Sufi poetry to wrap around him like a gossamer veil, soft and elusive. Each metaphor seeped into the crevices of his mind, breathing life into the solitary existence he led. A life spent retreating from the world, preferring the embrace of ink and parchment over the messy complexities of human connection.

As he translated intricate lines about the divine and the soul's yearning, he felt they resonated with a depth he had long avoided confronting. The poets spoke of love and longing as if they were waves crashing against the shores of their hearts, and in their words, he recognised his own isolation. The rhymes flowed like water, carving channels through the hard rock of his solitude, leaving behind echoes of emotions he had buried deep. With every stroke of his pen, Karim uncovered not just the meaning of the lines but a reflection of his own melancholic journey.

Yet as the poems deepened his emotional landscape, they also conjured a sense of urgency within him. What had once been a sanctuary became a prison of words. Beautiful, yes, but confining.

Fragments of his life outside the flat seeped into his consciousness, unruly and disruptive. The laughter of children playing in the Halfaouine district, the tantalising aromas wafting from nearby souks, the vibrant colours of the marketplace. These memories resurfaced like distant echoes, drowning beneath the weight of the verses he was translating.

Karim felt trapped in a paradox; the poetry offered him solace yet drew him closer to the precipice of a world he had forsaken. Were they merely whispers of the past, or did they beckon him towards something more tangible? He pondered whether each translated word was a step towards understanding himself, or an invitation to venture into the lively chaos he had long eluded.

As sunset bathed the city in a golden hue, light filtered through the dust-laden windows of his flat, illuminating the delicate calligraphy that lined the walls. Each ornate phrase glinted like the shifting sands of time, reminding him of both the transience and the permanence of his existence.

Thunder rumbled in the distance, the sound resembling whispers in a language he could almost understand. A forgotten line from a poem he once learned resounded within him:

"In every heartbeat lies the pulse of the universe."

With an electric thrill coursing through him, Karim realised that the night ahead would not simply be another chapter consumed in solitude. He could sense the arrival of something profound, promising yet fraught with uncertainty.

He closed the books and stood, the weight of unspoken emotions hanging heavily in the air, as shadows stretched toward him like fingers beckoning him forth. He felt the call reverberate, a silent urging to transcend the confines of translation to embrace the living poetry of life itself. As he stepped towards the door, the thought surfaced with haunting clarity: perhaps, hidden within the very fabric of Sufi poetry, lay a map not just of the city of Tunis, but of the uncharted landscapes of his heart.

Karim's apartment symbolised not just his

love for literature but also the profound solitude that enveloped him like the thick Tunisian air. Nestled in a corner of the bustling Halfaouine district, his small refuge overlooked the vibrant life below, yet it felt worlds apart. The walls were lined with shelves overflowing with dusty volumes of Sufi poetry, their spines cracked from years of gentle handling. The scent of ageing paper mingled with the faint aroma of oranges from the street vendors, creating a bittersweet atmosphere that completed Karim's isolation.

As he translated the intricate verses of long-forgotten poets, the ink danced beneath his fingers, whispering the language of desire, longing, and unfulfilled connections. Each line became a reminder of his reluctance to engage deeply with the world and the individuals that inhabited it. There was solace in the rhythm of the Sufi couplets—as if they understood his need for distance, yet beckoned him toward human connection all the same. Still, he pressed onward, frequently losing himself in the metaphysical worlds crafted by poets like Ibn Arabi and Rumi, where love transcended physical presence and solitude was celebrated as a divine state.

Throughout his days and late nights, Karim wrestled with conflicting emotions as he isolated himself further from the very essence of life that flowed so freely outside his window. His passion for literature provided a shield, a thick wall that separated him from the noise of human interactions. The residents below animated the streets with laughter, music, and conflict—elements of existence he found both fascinating and painfully out of reach. He held the poetry close, like a talisman, believing that through words and ink, he could understand the nuances of life, even if he never dared to fully embrace them. However, as the sun dipped below the horizon, casting long shadows across his walls, a creeping sense of urgency began to take hold. The whispers of the past, the resonant voices of Sufi poetry, urged him to forge a connection before the abyss of solitude consumed him whole.

That day, as he sat at the small wooden table illuminated by the flickering candlelight, he felt an anxiety swell within him, a pressure that waxed like the moon in the sky. Each moment without connection, each evening spent amidst the abandoned pages, intensified the weight of his solitude.

He closed his eyes and listened to the City breathe, the sounds a distant murmur—its life echoing of faded memories and unrealised follies. What, he pondered, would be left of him when he faded away into obscurity? The very thought struck a more resounding chord, sending chills down his spine. Would he be merely a shadow amongst the stories of others, a footnote in the grand narratives woven through his translations? The thought haunted him, intensifying his desire to break free from the chains of isolation that bound him.

With each passing hour, the urgency grew fiercer; cracks in the facade of his literary pursuits widened, revealing the chasm of loneliness that lay beneath. As night settled in and the lanterns flickered to life below, igniting the maze-like streets with scattered sparks, Karim knew this was a decision point.

His heart raced as he considered the faded text on the scattered papers of Horn strewn across his desk—a tapestry of the unknown, much like the fabric of his own life. He could continue to translate, to hide behind words and manuscripts, or he could dare to step outside, to reach for the living poetry of the world around him. With a final glance at the shadows dancing on his walls, he stood up, heart pounding, ready to confront what lay beyond. The whispers of the past had ignited a flame within, and he could no longer ignore it.

***

2
The Forgotten Villa

Karim stood at the entrance of the villa, the salty breeze from the sea weaving through the air, carrying with it whispers of the past. He had descended into the heart of forgotten splendour, where the remnants of Dr. Elias Horn's life lay entangled with dust and memories. As he cautiously stepped inside, the floor creaked beneath him, a muted echo of the once-vibrant life that had thrived here. Thick vines crept along the cracked walls, and shafts of sunlight streamed through shattered windows, illuminating motes of dust that danced like restless spirits.

It was not just the tranquil beauty of the decaying villa that piqued Karim's interest; it was the extraordinary potential hidden within its neglected corners. He had come searching for Horn's papers, whispered of in hushed tones, believing they held the keys to something profound—an understanding that transcended mere meteorological observations. As he sifted through old furniture and shifting shadows, his heartbeat quickened with the thrill of discovery.

He spotted an old wooden desk, its surface marred by time but still resolute in its purpose. With careful hands, he wiped away layers of dust, revealing a small stack of dishevelled papers bound by a frayed string. As he pulled them towards him, an unsettling sensation crept along his spine. The notes were not the dry records of weather patterns he had anticipated. Instead, they were a turbulent tapestry of fragmented thoughts. These intricate diagrams twisted and spiralled into one another like the labyrinthine paths of the Medina.

His breath caught as he absorbed the scribbles—wind patterns overlaid with maps, odd references to "Anemoi Mapping," which Horn proposed could chart not just physical winds, but the very currents of fate and memory within Tunis itself. The ink seemed to pulse beneath his fingertips, resonating with a truth he could scarcely comprehend. The possibilities unfurled within his mind, electrifying him with a sense of mission. Could it be that Horn had not simply vanished, but had perhaps unravelled the very fabric of reality through his explorations?

Karim's hands trembled as he delved deeper into the papers, each word acting as a thread pulling him further away from his mundane life and into a maelstrom of existential questions. As dusk settled, shadows lengthened, and the remnants of day faded into twilight, he felt the weight of secrecy pressing down on him. The scent of sea salt mingled with the mustiness of the villa, creating a sensory tapestry that linked him intimately to Horn's world. The deeper he plunged into the notes, the more he felt he was not merely an observer, but a participant in Horn's haunting, enigmatic journey.

Then, a sudden noise shattered the silence. A rustle from the far corner of the room. Karim's heart raced. Had someone else entered this forgotten space? Or was it merely the echoes of memories awakened by his presence? He stood frozen, body taut, every muscle urged to flee but grounded by insatiable curiosity. A shadow flitted past the doorway, disappearing before he could register its shape. Was it just a figment of his imagination, or something more ethereal? He gripped the papers tightly, feeling their significance coursing through him like an electric charge.

"If Horn's work is indeed alive," he murmured under his breath, "then perhaps his fate was intertwined with these very currents."

The thought both thrilled and terrified him as a sense of urgency surged within. He needed to understand, to pursue the trail of knowledge that Horn had left behind, and yet, something loomed on the horizon that warned him of the price of such knowledge. The flickering candle-light cast foreboding shadows around him, diluting the fatherly light of understanding with the ambiguity of dark consequence.

As the last vestiges of sunlight bled into the horizon, Karim made the choice before him:

continue unravelling Horn's tangled threads or retreat into the comfort of the known, away from the villa where past and present danced perilously close. The air grew thick with anticipation, urging him toward the enigmatic journey that awaited. A plunge into the unknown that promised enlightenment, yet whispered of madness. The echoes of Horn beckoned, and Karim felt himself teetering on the threshold of discovery, where every choice carved a path into an intricate labyrinth of existence.

***

The moment Karim crossed the threshold of Horn's villa, he was enveloped by the familiar yet foreign aroma. The mingled scent of sea salt and dust. It clung to the air like an old secret, whispering forgotten stories soaked in sunlight and decay. Each step further into the villa seemed to reverberate with the echoes of waves crashing against the rocky shore, distant yet ever-present, reminding him of the sea's relentless passage of time.

His senses heightened with every creak of the

wooden floorboards, as if they held the weight of myriad footsteps preceding him, each traced by a story lost to the ether. The sun filtered weakly through the remnants of cracked windowpanes, casting fragmented shadows that danced like spectres of the past. Dust motes hung suspended in the air, swirling lazily, intertwining with the salty breeze that drifted in from the open balcony. It wasn't just the villa's physical space that captivated him; it was the essence of Horn himself that seemed to permeate the walls, an invisible thread linking him to the absent figure of the vanished scholar.

As he wandered through the decaying grandeur, the juxtaposition of ocean spray and earthy particles led his mind deeper into contemplation. What mysteries lie beneath the surface of this fading beauty? The very air seemed to breathe a narrative of longing and abandon, a testament to Horn's obsession with understanding the 'Anemoi Winds'. The metaphysical currents connecting memory, fate, and the labyrinthine paths of Tunis.

Karim took a breath, letting the scent fill him, allowing it to sediment in his thoughts like the layers of dust coating the abandoned furniture. Each inhalation felt like an invocation, as if he were daring the villa to disclose its hidden truths. But the more he probed, the more he could sense an unyielding silence, a cautious whisper reminding him that not all questions welcomed an answer.

Nevertheless, intrigue ignited a flame within him, setting him on a path to extract the essence of Horn's inquiry as he sifted through scattered papers on the ageing oak desk. His fingers brushed against a yellowed manuscript, its contents offering dire hints about mapping not just the city's geography, but the labyrinthine pathways of the human soul.

Suddenly, an unexpected gust swept through the villa, rattling the shutters and causing a shiver to run down his spine. Was it the wind or something more? The scent shifted, becoming both heavy with urgency and exhilaratingly vibrant, urging him to peel back layers that had long been buried.

His heart raced as the idea emerged that perhaps Horn's disappearance was linked to a deeper truth, one that lurked just beyond the edge of his understanding. Was he ready to confront what lay buried not only within the dusty confines of this villa, but within his own reluctant heart? The tension thickened in the air like an impending storm. As shadows stretched and shifted, he felt unmoored, teetering on the brink of discovery. Yet, the very thought of unearthing the past set him reeling—what if the knowledge he sought was more than he could bear? As he held the manuscript close, the question loomed larger: Was he seeking the wisdom of Horn or merely inviting the whispers of the abyss to breathe into his soul?

As Karim sat on the faded velvet settee of the forgotten villa, the echoes of Dr. Horn's life loomed around him like shadows in the flickering candlelight. The musty smell of old paper and sea salt mingled with the dust motes hanging lazily in the afternoon sun. Horn's absence was palpable, an almost living entity that filled the room with an air of despair and wonder. Karim felt it seep into his bones, curling around his thoughts as he carefully unwrapped the stack of papers, each fragment a piece of a puzzle that seemed to breathe with mystery.

In his quest to unravel Horn's fate, Karim found himself entwined with the whispers of knowledge that rippled through the pages. The notes sketched out a labyrinthine map of currents. Not just of air or water, but of human experience, coloured by desire and fear, hope and loss. Each word carried a heavy implication that seeking truth was to risk disappearance, akin to stepping off an edge without knowing where one would land. He considered the price Horn might have paid, the knowledge he gained or lost in his obsession, and whether the pursuit of such understanding was worth the sacrifice of one's existence.

As twilight deepened outside, Karim's thoughts spiralled. The fading light played tricks upon the walls, making shapes out of the shadows that danced restlessly. He pondered the stories Horn had sought to tell, the threads of fate woven together beneath the surface of the apparent. What had driven Horn to the precipice of this metaphysical exploration? Karim's fingers traced the delicate curves of the old astrolabe, the flawed tool that Selma claimed could measure the inclination of whispers. He felt a shiver, realising he was standing at the edge of a chasm. A decision point where to leap in pursuit of Horn's legacy might take him to unimaginable places, perhaps to the same fate Horn himself had faced.

Karim's heart surged with a combination of dread and exhilaration. The underlying currents of Horn's notes beckoned him forward, each diagram more complex than the last, merging maps of wind with the vast, unpredictable landscape of the human soul. Suddenly, he caught a glimpse of movement in the corner of his eye. He turned, and for a fleeting moment, thought he saw a figure standing in the doorway, half-hidden in shadow, watching him with an intensity that electrified the air. But when he blinked, the figure was gone, leaving only a lingering echo of presence that rattled the silence.

Time stretched, and with it, the room felt as though it were shifting subtly around him, like the winds Horn had sought to chart. Doubts clawed at the edges of his mind. Was he chasing shadows, like the elusive Horn before him, or was he nearing a revelation? This was more than a mere academic pursuit; it was an exploration of existence itself.

As the sun dipped further below the horizon, a sense of urgency pulsed through him. Was it possible for him to follow Horn's path and emerge enlightened, or would he, too, be lost in the Anemoi currents, forever a ghost within the villa's abandoned halls? The weight of the unanswered questions pressed down on him, propelling him to move forward, into the unknown.

3

Maps of the Mind

As Karim delved deeper into the enigmatic world of Dr. Horn's papers, he found himself captivated by the alluring notion of 'Anemoi Mapping.' It was a concept as elusive as the winds themselves. This method supposedly charted not only the physical currents of air but also the currents of fate, memory, and potentiality layered within the fabric of Tunis. This mapping promised a dynamic interplay between perception and reality, where the observer became part of the observation.

Each fragment of Horn's notes drew him farther away from the mundanity of his life, whispering of a forgotten wisdom that resonated with the rhythm of the City. Karim roamed the labyrinthine streets of the Medina, each winding alley seeming to shift beneath his feet, reshaping his sense of direction and purpose. He felt as though he were walking amidst echoes of the past, the air thick with scents of jasmine and cumin. The deeper he ventured, the more tangible Horn's theories became, moulding the very essence of his experience. Yet, a nagging doubt clawed at the edges of his mind: was he losing himself in this pursuit, or was he on the brink of an extraordinary revelation?

Days turned to weeks as he began to construct his own 'Anemoi Map,' tracing connections between Horn's scribbles and his own memories. At each location he visited, elements of his past intertwined with the present, sending shivers down his spine. Standing at a forgotten fountain tucked away in a narrow alley, he sensed old voices whispering lost verses from the Sufi poetry he so loved. Was it a figment of his imagination, or truly the City breathing life into his recollections? Each visit felt like a riddle, leading him closer to a truth he could not yet comprehend.

Her shop, cluttered with forgotten relics, felt like the heart of the city, its walls steeped in the wisdom of ages. She studied him with eyes that seemed to pierce through his earthly concerns, her voice a melodic whisper as she spoke of the shifting winds. These were not just the physical winds that blew through the City, but the metaphorical winds of change, of fate and destiny. Not all who chart the Anemoi roads return unchanged, Karim, she warned cryptically. Some maps lead into the depths of the soul, where reality and delusion entwine.

The plight of knowing swept over him, propelling him toward a precipice he could not ignore. At dusk, with the shadows lengthening and the winds rising, he stood at the edge of the Lake of Tunis, Horn's final convergence point looming before him. A promise of clarity mingled with fear bubbles in his chest as the lunar glow illuminates the water. Beyond the surface shimmered glimpses of countless possibilities. At that moment, Karim felt the weight of his choices heavy upon his shoulders. Should he complete the map, diving deeper into the unknown, or shatter it, preserving the sanctity of his reality? The winds screamed for him to decide.

With the last soft hues of twilight bleeding into night, Karim took a determined step toward the lake, driven by a desire to unveil the truth, yet unaware of the transformative journey that awaited him. The air thickened with anticipation, tinged with both danger and beauty, threatening to consume him whole as he prepared to cast his fate into the wild currents of the Anemoi.

Karim sat alone in his dimly lit flat, the sounds of the Halfaouine district drifting through the cracked window. The pages before him were filled with Dr. Horn's scrawled notes, fragments of thoughts weaving an intricate tapestry of curiosity and despair. The concept of 'Anemoi Mapping' hung in the air like an unfurling scroll, teasing the boundaries of his understanding and drawing him deeper into Horn's enigmatic world.

As he pieced together the fragments, he felt the edges of his own memories blur, the past melding with the present. Each note resonated with echoes of forgotten conversations, whispers of poetry that floated in and out of his mind like fog rolling over the City at dawn. The connection between his solitude and Horn's theories began to crystallise; both men were seekers navigating the labyrinth of memory and identity, searching for a way to chart the invisible currents that shaped their lives.

With each passing moment, Karim felt the pull of the Medina, its labyrinthine alleys calling him to walk the paths that Horn had once explored. He recalled a moment from his childhood, the scent of jasmine mingling with spices, guiding him down a narrow street. Had he stumbled upon a memory, or was it merely a fleeting vision conjured by the pages in front of him? The idea ignited within him a fragile hope that perhaps he could unlock the secrets buried within the City's veins.

Suddenly, the threads of reality began to fray.

The flickering candlelight cast shadows that twisted and danced along the walls, breathing life into the indecipherable outlines of figures he thought he had left behind. He could almost hear the voices of past lovers and friends whispering to him from the corners of his mind, their words laced with the bittersweet cadence of nostalgia. In his quest to understand Horn's theories, Karim felt as if he were reaching beyond the veil of time, intertwining his own longing with the rich tapestry of those who came before him.

He suppressed the creeping dread that accompanied such realisations. The fear that perhaps, in pursuing Horn's insights, he risked losing his own identity entirely. However, that fear only fuelled his obsession. The fragments of memory within Horn's notes began to morph and expand, whispering of intersections where the past and present met, urging him further along the precarious path of discovery.

As twilight descended, a chill swept through the air, carrying with it the scent of rain mingling with the cosiness of roasted chestnuts. This aroma ignited memories of fleeting connections and laughter in the bustling souks. Karim closed his eyes, envisioning a world that stretched beyond the confines of his flat. In this world, the rain masked the boundaries of time, allowing him to step into the echoes of yesterday's conversations.

Driven by the urgency of his quest, he clasped the papers. He rose, the decision coarse upon his tongue. He would not merely translate Horn's words. Still, he would venture out into the Medina, following the trails marked within the fragments of his own memory. Tonight he would attempt to weave together the disparate threads of the past, to understand not only Horn's fate but his own.

But as he stepped into the uncertainty of the night, a gust of wind swept through the alleyways, wrapping around him like a whispered promise, urging him to follow its direction. Each breath he took resonated with the notion that perhaps knowledge didn't lie in the pages of fragmented postings but in the very act of living, of connecting the disparate, the ephemeral, and the eternal. The path lay before him, undoubtedly rife with danger but illuminated by an undeniable allure. He could feel his pulse quicken at the thought of discovery.

With heart racing and senses heightened, Karim embarked on a journey that could unravel the threads binding him to the present or shatter the very essence of his existence as he knew it. The winds of the Medina beckoned, and with them, the whispers of memory that would guide his footsteps deeper into the unknown.

***

As Karim sat in his modest flat, surrounded by books and manuscripts, he pondered
the essence of translation itself. To him, each
word was a map, a labyrinth of meaning that
shifted and transformed under the weight of
cultural context. Sufi poetry, with its intricate
metaphors and allusions to the divine, offered a
unique challenge. It wasn't merely about trans-
mitting words from one language to another;
it was about capturing the essence, the emo-
tion that breathed life into those words. In this
process, he often felt more like a cartographer
than a translator, charting the uncharted territories of his own mind as he navigated the
dense thickets of spirituality within the texts.

Karim's fingers traced the frayed edges of
a translated verse, where he had struggled
to find the perfect equivalent for a single
word that carried layers of cultural significance.
He recognised that translation, much like the
Anemoi Mapping he was now grappling with,
was a living thing, dynamic and responsive to
the winds of change. As he delved deeper into
his task, he began to see parallels between the

ancient maps of Carthage and the poetic lines unfolding before him. Both sought to capture the intangible, guiding those who dared to wander off the well-trodden paths. Each map could lead one to unseen realms, just as every poem could reveal startling truths about the human experience.

But the deeper he ventured into this labyrinth of language and meaning, the more he felt its pull toward an unknown. He sensed the echoes of Dr. Horn's lost research mingling with his own thoughts, urging him to question if translation could unlock help in deciphering the City's shifting realities. With each translated line of poetry, a subtle chaos began to whisper at the edges of his mind, hinting that perhaps the words he was translating were not merely reflections of a singular knowledge, but doorways to something far more profound. In the rare silence of his flat, Karim began to understand that he was not just a translator of texts; he was also the architect of his own evolving map, and that the choices he made, that the interpretations he brought forth, could resonate through the very fabric of time and memory.

Yet, an uneasy tension lingered in the air, thickening as he grappled with the truth of his exploring thoughts. If the translations he crafted held power beyond mere expression, what price might he pay for this newfound understanding? As if in response to his contemplation, a draft swept through the open window, carrying with it a hint of jasmine from the neighbouring gardens, mingled with the musty aroma of ancient pages. It was a reminder of the City outside, a realm steeped in secrets and shadows, where each alley could morph into treachery, and each turn of phrase bore the weight of destiny.

As Karim leaned closer to his work, an overwhelming urge ignited in him. A desire not only to translate these Sufi verses but to live them, to breathe their wisdom as he embarked on his own journey through the secret contours of Tunis. With that desire swelling in his chest, he knew he could no longer merely interpret the maps of others; he must forge his own path entirely, through the entwined worlds of language and fate, where every decision could lead to enlightenment or possibly madness. At that moment, the tension crackled in the air, urging him forward, toward whatever awaited him in the labyrinthine depths of the Medina.

***

4

The Labyrinth of the Medina

The sounds of the lively chorus of voices, the aromas of freshly baked bread blending with spices, and the rainbow of colours surrounded Karim like a complex tapestry as he entered the Medina. He was on a quest to understand the fragmented notes of Dr. Horn, a scholar who had delved into the city's metaphysical currents. The souks thrummed with a life of their own, each twist and turn of the narrow alleyways echoing the labyrinthine thoughts swirling in his mind. These bustling avenues, both familiar and foreign, felt alive, as if they were shifting under his very feet, guiding him deeper into their concealed recesses.

He moved past stalls adorned with brass lanterns and intricate carpets, the vendors' calls punctuating the air with an inviting urgency. Yet, as he wandered, shadows of doubt crept in, whispering questions about his quest for understanding the fragmented notes of Dr. Horn. Did he merely chase the ghost of a man who might have lost himself in the very depths of this maze? The realisation gnawed at him, transforming excitement into a tight coil of anxiety. The Medina, with its hidden passages and cryptic warnings, was a place of mystery and danger.

Suddenly, a scent lodged itself in his consciousness, a fleeting yet potent mix of jasmine and something distinctly oceanic. It urged him toward a hidden passage, barely wide enough for a man to squeeze through. The mystery of this passage wrestled with his curiosity. Yet, he pressed on, feeling a strange compulsion to follow the path where the air thickened and the atmosphere shifted. A flickering lantern ahead promised revelations, but also hinted at dangers lurking within the shadows.

Karim's heart raced as he entered a quieter nook of the Medina, where the bustling energy seemed to retreat, replaced by an unsettling stillness. The walls, once vibrant, wore a veil of dust, and the forging of memories felt stagnant in the air. An old woman hobbled by, her eyes glinting with a knowing, unsettling familiarity. You seek maps of the winds, but the winds can be treacherous, she offered cryptically, her voice an echo mixed with the rustle of old pages. He shivered, feeling the gravity of her words pull at the edges of his resolve.

Gazing around, Karim sensed he was not merely a visitor in this space but rather a participant in an age-old dance of destiny. With each step, the souk's spirals seemed to entangle him in history's threads. Here, truth blurred into illusion, and the past whispered riddles in his ear. The surrounding labyrinth pulsated, bearing witness to seekers who had wandered before him, some who had returned, others who remained lost like Dr. Horn. The Medina was not just a physical place, but a crucible of self-discovery.

His thoughts spiralled with the shifting narrative of his journey. Was Horn a scholar unravelling the city's metaphysical currents, or had he succumbed to the very depths of madness? These questions echoed through Karim's mind as he turned a corner, and suddenly, the atmosphere thickened, charged with an electric tension that stilled his breath. Ahead, he spotted an ornate fountain, one he'd noted on Horn's maps. The water danced with a luminous quality, casting ephemeral reflections that beckoned him closer. Perhaps this place will unveil the secrets I seek.

As he approached the fountain, he recalled Selma bin Hazm's warnings about the dangers buried within knowledge. The shimmering water mesmerised him, and for an instant, he felt entwined in its flow, a part of the ever-shifting currents. Yet, a chill prickled his skin, pulling him back from the brink. What if this were a glimpse into a deeper truth, or perhaps a mirage that seduced explorers into oblivion? The question reverberated in his chest, each beat a cautious reminder that to venture further might lead him to where reality itself unravelled.

Before he could ponder any longer, a sharp sound broke the trance. A whispering breeze swept through, carrying fragmented voices from behind him, merging the past and present into a single murmur. Turned, Karim could make out figures moving just beyond the fountain's shimmering depths, ghostly apparitions, faces he almost recognised, caught in a moment between the worlds they occupied. His heart thundered, the air thickening into an urgent plea. You must choose, Karim. Dare you follow? The tension in the air was palpable, a weight on his shoulders as he contemplated his next move.

As Karim navigated the intricate passages of the Medina, a world of aromatic contrasts enveloped him. The rich, earthy scents of spices from the souk melded with the sharpness of mint and the heady fragrance of jasmine, casting an invisible net that caught his senses. Each turn he made drew him deeper into a peripheral existence, as if the labyrinth itself orchestrated a symphony of scents meant to guide his revelations. The air thickened with histories interwoven within these odours, each telling a story that resonated with his growing obsession.

In the depths of the Souk el-Attarine, surrounded by countless vials of perfume, Karim felt himself drawn to a particular aroma, faint yet intoxicating—a brush of citrus mingled with the dust of antiquity. It was then that he recalled Horn's notes, which hinted at specific scents as keys to perceiving the metaphysical layers of the city. The fleeting notes of something familiar tugged at his memory, compelling him to grasp the intangible threads connecting his reality and Horn's elusive theories. The essence seemed to whisper secrets of the past, sending tremors of understanding coursing through his veins as he drew in a deep breath.

The idea that scent could hold potential truths began to galvanise his imagination. If the city could be mapped not only through physical dimensions but through ephemeral trails of fragrance, what could he uncover? He envisioned the scents imprinted on his growing Anemoi Map, marking the places and moments where he would most likely encounter revelations. Not only about Horn, but about himself. The frantic heartbeat of the City around him faded as he delved into this aromatic reverie, revealing the delicate connections between the material and the metaphysical.

Continuing through the Medina, Karim found himself at a crossroads, a place where the scents converged with an almost orchestrated precision. A rich perfume of fig swirled with the sharpness of cardamom, whilst far to his left came the angry, salty tang of the sea. Each of these signals began to form an impression on his mind, resonating with the echo of Horn's voice speaking of 'Anemoi Mapping'. It was here, structured by the very atmosphere of scents, that he felt a kaleidoscope of destiny unfurl before him. Yet, amidst the fragrant tapestry, an undercurrent of tension tinged the air, a sense of foreboding mixed with discovery, as if the city itself was warning him to tread carefully.

As he pressed further along the alley, a sudden gust whipped through the outskirts of the souk, stirring the sensory landscape into chaos. The metamorphic winds carried scents both familiar and foreign. In the swirl of fragrances, Karim felt a profound shift, as if the very fabric of reality pressed against him, demanding release. There was a moment of clarity amidst the intoxicating whirlwind: memories of the figures he had glimpsed in the labyrinth resurfaced. Shadows flickered at the edges of his vision, reminiscent of witnesses from another time. Were they the echoes of those who had sought the same path as Horn and lost themselves in the blurring boundaries of the city's scent-bound labyrinth?

Suddenly, a familiar yet hauntingly elusive voice floated through the air. A line from the Sufi poetry he had once translated, echoing seamlessly within the fragrance-laden winds, its tone imbued with a sense of urgency. This was not simply the past repeating; it held an invitation, a challenge. Karim's heart raced as he realised he could not just observe, but had to engage. The imperfections of Horn's map began to crystallise into a deeper understanding. He was part of this labyrinth, part of its pulse. But as the scents intensified, so did the weight of his choices. Would he pursue the path Horn had tread, aware of the fine line between enlightenment and madness that existed in the folds of these fragrant currents?

As the paths shifted beneath his feet, Karim stood at a precipice, the myriad of scents swirling around him. Time felt thin, and the world grew both vibrant and menacing. Each scent held a key, a response intertwined with his fate. Yet, an unsettling thought weighed heavily upon him: what if deciphering these olfactory mysteries led him not to understanding but to eternal entrapment? With the shadowy figures lingering at the fringe of his perception, he braced himself: with one hand tethered to the fading threads of Horn's legacy and the other reaching for the labyrinth's elusive brush of scent-filled reality.

The winding alleys of the Medina whispered secrets, their uneven cobblestones a gentle reminder of the paths less travelled. As Karim meandered through stalls laden with spices and textiles, he couldn't shake the sensation that the walls themselves were watching, shifting ever so subtly in the background of his consciousness. Each curve and corner felt alive, as if the very essence of the city was scrutinising his intent, mapping out the intersection of fate and perception.

With each fleeting scent, the heady aroma of jasmine mingling with the dust of ancient tomes, Karim found echoes of Horn's theories reverberating within him. The souks became a tapestry of sensory experiences; each sound and smell was a thread woven into the fabric of his reality. Yet, he sensed a growing tension in this woven narrative, an undercurrent of something just beyond his grasp. Was it merely the thrill of discovery, or did the Medina guard some deeper truth, pressing against the boundaries of his understanding?

As he ventured deeper into the labyrinth, a haven of shadows and flickering lanterns, Karim stumbled into a hidden courtyard where the air was thick with mystery. Here, he believed, lay the crux of Horn's designs, a place where metaphysical winds converged. Heart racing, he pulled out the tattered map, its edges frayed from relentless searching and hopeful skirmishes with fate. He illuminated specific markings with trembling fingers, feeling the pull of the unseen that encircled his thoughts and ambitions like a noose. What lay at the heart of this equation he had inadvertently set into motion? Was he merely a translator of Horn's echoes, or had he become a player on this stage of swirling perceptions?

And then, with unexpected urgency, he overheard a conversation drifting through the air. A pair of merchants discussing not wares, but whispers of an old legend surrounding the very souk in which he stood. Their words ignited something primal inside him: the suggestion that the Medina was alive, possessing the ability to reflect one's inner turmoil and desires. The realisation struck him like a bolt. Had he facilitated his own maze, constructing walls of perception that now enclosed him? How could he escape the very labyrinth he was aiming to map?

The intensity of the moment crescendoed when he caught sight of a flicker. A figure silhouetted against the backdrop of the bustling souk. Startled yet captivated, Karim moved closer, feeling an inexplicable pull. The figure wore a tattered cloak reminiscent of those worn by old Sufi scholars. Yet, their face was obscured, drawing him further into the heart of confusion and curiosity. Was this a manifestation of Medina's wisdom, or merely a spectre of his own unravelling thoughts?

Just as he reached for the shadowy outline, the crowd surged, swaying like the wind that Horn had so frequently referenced. Voices blurred into a cacophony, engulfing him. Thoughts cascaded. Questions unanswered. Was he on the verge of unveiling some essential truth, or had his pursuit turned against him, revealing the limitations of his understanding?

Suddenly, the air thickened, and he felt the weight of the city pressing down, the atmosphere charged with an unseen energy that threatened to either reveal the mysteries he sought or plunge him into a deeper abyss of madness. When he looked again, the figure had vanished, slipping through the fold of the labyrinthine paths like a memory dissolving in the grip of time.

At that moment, the urgency settled in his bones. The convergence Horn had spoken of loomed ahead, a threshold beyond which lay the unknown, and Karim grasped that simply mapping the winds would not suffice. There was a choice to make: to embrace the unknown paths ahead, or retreat into his familiar solitude. The echoes in the Medina pressed against his mind, each whisper urging him to either leap or cower in the shadows.

***

5

Selma bin Hazm's Riddles

Karim pushed open the creaking door of Selma bin Hazm's antique shop, stepping into an embrace of dust and time. The air was thick with the scent of old leather, spices, and a hint of jasmine that seemed to linger in the corners like a whispered promise. The shop, a treasure trove of age-worn trinkets and oddities, held an unexplainable allure, beckoning Karim deeper into its mysterious depths.

Selma, a figure woven from the fabric of memories, regarded him with eyes that sparkled with untold stories. She stood behind a counter cluttered with an array of relics: chipped ceramics, faded textiles, and brass astrolabes that appeared to dance in the light filtering through the time-stained windows. Her presence exuded profound wisdom, a knowledge of the ages that piqued Karim's curiosity.

"You seek what is hidden," she said, her voice a melodic riddle, "but beware. The treasure you find may consume your very essence."

As she spoke, the ambience shifted, and Karim could almost hear the gentle murmurs of the City outside, as if the walls were alive with the memory of its inhabitants. He felt the weight of Selma's gaze, the depth of knowledge cloaked in her playful riddles.

"To listen to the City's breath," she continued, her fingers tracing the rim of a dusty astrolabe, "is to understand its secrets. But know this: some maps chart territories from which you cannot return."

Her words carried a weight of danger, a sense of foreboding that added a thrilling edge to Karim's exploration.

Intrigued yet apprehensive, Karim angled closer as Selma unveiled an ancient brass instrument, its surface battered but still gleaming with a haunting allure.

"This is a map of whispers," she explained, the astrolabe embodying the imperfections of knowledge and perception. "It charts not the stars, but the souls that roam this labyrinthine City, echoes of whom you must hear if you wish to navigate your fate."

He reached out, the cool metal feeling foreign against his fingertips, a tingle of both danger and exhilaration coursing through him.

"What if I find something I cannot comprehend?" Karim whispered.

Selma's smile deepened, a knowing crease at the corners of her eyes.

"Ah, my dear translator, there lies the crux of it all."

The shelves seemed to shift slightly as the astrolabe fell from his grip, spiralling downwards.

In that heart-stopping moment, the whispers of the City intensified, swirling around him like a tempest. Karim caught glimpses of twisted alleyways that had never existed before, and flickering shadows of figures long gone danced at the periphery of his vision.

"You must choose, Karim," Selma urged, her voice now a shadow itself, reverberating with urgency. "The City has its own agenda, and time ebbs and flows like the tides."

Karim's heart raced as he contemplated the stories woven into the depths of Selma's shop. The antique relics bore witness to countless lifetimes and secrets, each possessing the potential to unravel or bind him. The astrolabe lay at his feet, its mechanism still whispering of knowledge gained and lost. In that charged air, with the City breathing around him, he sensed the urge to follow the map of whispers. Whether he would emerge enlightened or ensnared loomed ominously over his every thought.

***

Selma bin Hazm's shop was a labyrinth unto itself, each shelf brimming with relics whispering tales from forgotten centuries. The dim light flickered against dusty artefacts, casting shadows that danced like spectres across the walls. As Karim entered, he felt an invisible weight, an atmosphere thick with secrets and unspoken truths. The delicate tinkling of a wind chime broke the heavy silence, and Selma looked up from behind a counter cluttered with faded textiles and chipped ceramics, her eyes shimmering with ancient wisdom and mischief.

Welcome, seeker of whispers, she greeted, her voice a melodic blend of age and grace. Have you come to listen? Karim stood still, the resonance of her inquiry echoing within him. He nodded, sensing he had stepped into a space where the essence of the City pulsed like a living entity, waiting for him to attune to its subtle rhythms. It was here that he would learn the art of perceiving the City's breath. Its ebb and flow, its quiet revelations.

Selma guided him to a small, intricately carved wooden chair in the corner of the shop. Sit and listen closely, she instructed, her demeanour both gentle and commanding. The City speaks in murmurs and sighs, and it is in these sounds that you may discover the paths unseen. Karim leaned back, closing his eyes, attuning himself to the myriad sounds spilling in from the bustling streets beyond the shop's threshold. The distant clatter of carts, the rhythmic calls of vendors, and the rustling of fabric as passersby brushed against the walls of the Medina.

As he sat immersed in the symphony of the City, it dawned on him that each sound was not merely noise, but a thread woven into the fabric of Tunisian life. A medium connecting the past to its present. Can you hear the jasmine blooming in the air? Selma asked, her voice pulling him from his reverie. It carries the whispers of lovers and poets, bridging the gap between what has been and what is yet to come. Karim inhaled deeply, the scent of jasmine intertwining with the salt of the sea, a haunting note of nostalgia tugging at the corners of his consciousness.

Selma continued, her words weaving a tapestry of interconnectedness that stirred something deep within him. Every alley has a story, every corner a riddle. As the winds shift, so too do the paths of those who walk these streets. Listen to their tales; only then can you find your own. Karim's heart raced as he considered her implications. If he could harmonise with the City's breath, perhaps Horn's enigmatic theories would dissolve into clarity, revealing not only the discourse of the town, but also his place within it.

Yet beneath the serene surface of Selma's wisdom lay an unsettling current, a hint of danger intertwined with enlightenment. But remember, seeker, Selma cautioned, her gaze sharp as a blade, some maps chart territories from which one cannot return. The deeper you delve into these whispers, the more they may ensnare you. A chill crept down his spine, and somewhere in the recesses of his mind, doubts began to intertwine with his ambition.

Karim's pulse quickened; he sensed a reckoning approaching. This dance with the City's breath was not merely an exploration but a tightrope walk between revelation and peril. As the clamour of the town outside seemed to crescendo, he felt a stirring within himself that promised discovery but threatened to plunge him into depths he might not be able to navigate. The balance of ambition and caution swayed precariously beneath him. Would he emerge with the truths he sought, or would he find himself lost, swallowed by the very mysteries he yearned to decode?

At that moment, the air around him grew dense, charged with possibility, and he understood that Selma's riddles were but the beginning of a journey that could alter the course of his existence. The weight of her warnings pressed heavily, intertwining with a growing desire to uncover the City's hidden maps, to draw the lines that converged upon his destiny. With the City's breath echoing in his ears, Karim realised he stood at the precipice of an unknown horizon, teetering between the safe confines of his reality and the boundless uncertainties that awaited him.

***

As Karim entered Selma bin Hazm's antique shop, the air thickened, swirling with dust motes that danced lazily in the sunbeams filtering through the grime-streaked glass. Each object on the creaking shelves seemed to hum with forgotten stories, longing to be heard. Yet, among the faded textiles and chipped ceramics, one item stood out. A tarnished astrolabe, its intricate designs marred by the passage of time. Selma, her silver hair framing her wizened face, watched Karim with an intensity that suggested she eagerly awaited his reaction.

Ah, the astrolabe, she said softly, her voice a melodic echo. It measures the inclination of whispers, yet is imperfect in its purpose, just as we are. Karim felt a shiver. He reached out, the cool metal sending a pulse through his fingers. The astrolabe's surface glimmered, revealing inscriptions that blurred the boundary between science and divination. It was as if the device were whispering secrets, inviting him into its arcane dance of navigation and fate.

Selma smiled knowingly. This ancient instrument was crafted not merely to chart the stars, but to unravel the very fabric of knowledge and perception. What do we map, but the contours of our understanding, which often lead us astray? Karim, drawn deeper into her world of riddles, held the astrolabe closer, its flawed craftsmanship humming with promise. He felt a magnetic pull toward its mysterious purpose, a yearning to grasp the threads of reality twisting in the air around him.

Yet, a nagging doubt clouded his thoughts. Could this faulty astrolabe become a mere echo of his own flawed perceptions? Was he destined to misunderstand Horn's theories, to lose himself navigating a labyrinth of half-truths and myths? As Karim pondered these questions, the rush of the City outside melded with Selma's voice. *Remember, not everyone who seeks knowledge finds clarity. Some paths lead only to shadows, entangled with despair.* The weight of her words pressed down on him, a dire warning tinged with an urgency that sent prickles of anxiety racing down his spine.

Yet, he remained entranced, the astrolabe a beacon of possibility promising some glimpse of more profound truths. Just as he was about to surrender to its call, a sudden gust of wind surged through the shop, extinguishing the feeble flame of the oil lamp resting on Selma's desk. Darkness enveloped the room, and silence fell like a shroud; the soft thrum of the City was held in collective suspense.

Karim's heart raced, and he clutched the astrolabe tighter, the sudden stillness brewing an unsettling tension. He could hear strange echoes in the silence, whispers that tugged at his consciousness, taunting him with half-formed insights on what lay ahead.

"Selma?" he called out, his voice wavering.

There was no answer, and the air thickened, suffocating him with uncertainty.

Swallowing hard, Karim staggered back, re-aligning himself with the slant of light filtering through gaps in the shutters. When Selma's presence re-emerged from the shadows, her expression was unreadable, and a veil of secrecy masked her gaze.

"Do you wish to chart your course, Karim?" She asked. "But be warned, there are maps from which one does not return."

His breath hitched at her ominous declaration, and the weight of the astrolabe in his hands suddenly felt like a reckoning. Was he prepared to confront the uncertain depths of Horn's legacy, or was he inviting madness upon himself?

In the lingering darkness, the tension coiled around him like a tightening noose, whispering promises and threats simultaneously. The choice loomed like an uncharted path ahead, teetering on the edge of reality and illusion. Karim knew he stood on the precipice of understanding. Yet, one misstep could plunge him into the abyss of a fate he could neither foresee nor control.

***

6

The Tide and Time

The horizon appeared to bend and shimmer as Karim stood on the deteriorating jetty that overlooked the crashing waves of La Marsa, a mirage taunting him with secrets that were just out of reach. The sun dipped low in the sky, casting a golden glow on the water, yet all he could focus on were the fragmented notes of Dr. Horn, his mentor and guide, swirling in his mind. Each scribbled word became a curious echo in the wind, teasing him with the promise of revelation while evading his grasp like an elusive breeze.

In the distance, the outline of the horizon merged into a blurred line, a perpetual division between the known world and the vast, un-charted territory of Horn's theories. Karim re-called the map, the intricate diagrams that bled lines of possibility into the very fabric of Tunis's geography. He felt a potent urgency, a tempest within him mirroring the unpredictable waves crashing against the jetty, rejecting the calm he yearned for. The allure of the unknown, the uncharted territory of Horn's theories, was a siren's call he couldn't resist.

As the Sirocco began to stir, bringing with it a swirling tang of salt and spice, Karim's heartbeat quickened. The wind invoked a chilling sense of recognition, drawing forth memories long buried like driftwood washed ashore. Each gust carried whispers of past voices. The lonely recitations of Sufi poetry mingling with the stirring sound of the town, creating a symphony of longing and the possibility of lost connections, particularly with his deceased father. The city felt alive, breathing with memories, and Karim couldn't shake the feeling that it was both enticingly familiar and chillingly foreign.

He shut his eyes for a moment, allowing the Sirocco to wrap around him, as if it were coaxing him to delve deeper into the labyrinth of time and perception that Horn had hinted at. This concept examines the subjective nature of reality and the impact of memory on our perception of the world. It was here, on this cusp where land met sea, that he might confront not only the figure of Horn, lost to the shadows of his own obsession, but also the swirling tides of his own destiny. Would he dare navigate this maelstrom, knowing that within it lay the power to alter the very map of his reality?

With each tumultuous wave crashing against the jetty, it felt less like a barrier and more like an invitation. For the first time, the thrill of exploration clashed against the weight of uncertainty. Karim realised that to follow Horn's path would require him to abandon the shores of normalcy. As the Sirocco howled in crescendo, urging him closer to the edge, Karim grasped his own makeshift map, its edges fluttering like nervous wings. Could their converging winds lead him to clarity, or only drown him in chaos?

As the horizon wavered and twisted before him, Karim sensed that time itself was reaching out to him through the tumult. An invisible thread connecting the past to the present, whispering promises of an answer long sought. The air thickened with possibility, each gust inviting him to either leap forward into the unknown or retreat to the familiar safety of his daily life. Yet, the tide was turning, and at that moment of balancing perilously on the edge of choice, Karim felt the stirring call of an adventure that would either guide him to unfathomable insights or drown him in the depths of madness.

As Karim stood on the windswept shoreline

of La Marsa, an unsettling unease crept into the marrow of his bones. The sunlight shimmered upon the waves, igniting a tempest of memories within him. He could feel them swirling like the sea, caught in the grip of a storm that had yet to arrive. With every breath, the cool air carried the scent of salt and nostalgia, bringing forth fragments of his past that lay buried beneath the weight of daily existence. The weight of his memories was a burden he couldn't shake.

He recalled an afternoon in his childhood, a day much like this one, when the skies had darkened unexpectedly. The clouds raced, racing against time, dragging with them a chorus of winds that danced around him like old friends. His mother had spoken of weather as if it were a living entity, each change in temperature reflecting not just the world outside, but the emotions nestled within their hearts.

"Storms are memories," she had said. "And calm days, they are the moments that linger, perfectly encapsulated."

Now, as he traced the intricate patterns of Horn's notes with his eyes, he understood all too well the connection between weather patterns and memory. The shifts in climate had a peculiar way of dredging up long-forgotten sentiments. These awakening feelings had been dulled by time. The impending Sirocco stirred something akin to fear within him, not just for the chaotic winds that would follow, but for what memories would surface, for what unbidden revelations lay in waiting. The weather, like a master puppeteer, was shaping his thoughts and memories.

The ocean roared a warning as dark clouds gathered on the horizon, imposing yet ominous. Karim recalled Horn's theories, how he believed that weather was an embodiment of knowledge, and how the very air encasing Tunis was a repository of emotional truths. Could it be that storms carried the burden of lost opportunities, while clear skies offered promise? As the winds began to twist and turn, Karim closed his eyes. He surrendered to the rush of fragrant sea air, each gust drawing forth tales woven into the very fabric of the city's history.

Shouts from the fishermen echoed through the air, their nets poised to dance once more at the edge of uncertainty. Karim's heart thrummed wildly; the tension mirrored the agitated surfaces of the waves. Was it merely the weather, or did the atmosphere carry whispers from the past, urging him to consider his own path? With each gust, he felt a weight-bearing down upon him, an invitation to confront his memories and examine the choices he had made, each intertwined with the city and Horn's legacy.

As the first drop of rain fell, painting the dry sand, he felt a shift; a memory brushed across his consciousness. A hidden trail in the Medina, a disheartening conversation with Selma. What had she said about the difficulty of unseen maps? He recalled the strange sense of time folding in on itself during those labyrinthine strolls. The walls of the Medina seemed to pulsate with life as the storm brewed above, drawing his own tangled memories into focus, shaping new truths he had yet to confront.

Feeling buoyed by both fear and exhilaration, Karim realised that in seeking Horn's hidden knowledge, he had inadvertently unearthed his own emotional records, each echoing back at him through the storm's fury. The winds entwined with the clouds mirrored the contours of his soul, leaving him at the precipice of discovery. Was he ready to embrace the confrontations this weather bore? Was he prepared to navigate his own emotional tempest while unravelling the mysteries Horn had left behind?

Thunder rumbled in the distance as if in response to his internal storm, and he understood this was no ordinary weather front. The air thickened with anticipation, as memories intertwined with the weight of knowledge stretched before him like the endless horizon. All around him, La Marsa transformed, revealed beneath the tumult of clouds; here stood a crucible of time, where he must face the answers lurking beneath the surface. Here, as the winds howled like ancient spirits, he would discover whether he could navigate the storm or would succumb to the very memories he sought to unravel.

As the sun dipped behind the horizon, a warm breath of the Sirocco wind whispered through La Marsa, wrapping itself around Karim like a ghostly shroud. He stood on the decaying jetty, the planks creaking beneath his weight, a symphony of wood and time calling out the secrets it had witnessed. The air was thick with the scent of sea salt and jasmine. This intoxicating blend recalled forgotten memories and layered meanings. The wind rustled his papers, sending his carefully arranged notes spiralling into chaos, yet within that chaos, he felt a strange sense of clarity.

The Sirocco was notorious. A tempest that carried not just heat, but also stories from distant lands. It swirled with the weight of history and the lightness of hope. Karim's mind raced as he recalled Dr. Horn's musings about the winds of fate, how they twisted through the narrow alleys of the Medina, reshaping his reality with each gust. He realised that this wasn't just a weather pattern; it was a harbinger of change. The air crackled with possibility, and a strange sense of urgency welled within him. He had to follow Horn's map, translate not just the words of the past but the essence of the air itself.

At that moment, Karim breathed in deeply, allowing the Sirocco to fill his lungs, bridging the gap between the tangible and the unseen. Every scent, every whisper from the wind resonated within him, amplifying emotions he had long buried. He envisioned Horn standing here years ago, maybe with the same thoughts flickering in his mind, pondering the confluence of time and choice. What if the wind could reveal more than just paths? What if it could reveal truths long hidden, metaphysical currents connecting past, present, and future? The weight of knowledge pressed down on him as a faint, nebulous figure flitted out of the corner of his eye, layered against the golden hues fading into twilight.

Instinctively, Karim turned his gaze, but the figure vanished like a mirage. Doubt crept in, amplified by the wind's ghostly tendrils: Was he chasing shadows, or had he, like Horn, become entwined within the very fabric of the city's essence? He felt the Sirocco urge him forward, meeting the unknown like a long-lost friend. Steeling himself, he clutched the notes tighter as if they were a lifeline. The realisation washed over him; whatever Horn had discovered out there, it drew closer, inviting him to confront the storm brewing within, a tempest of knowledge that dared to unspool before him.

With the wind swirling around him, Karim began to walk toward the hidden pathways that Horn had mapped but never completed. He knew now that to pursue that knowledge, to join the ranks of those who had dared to chart the unchartable, he must surrender to the Sirocco's embrace, accepting the duality of creation and destruction, revelation and madness. As shadows danced along the alleys, the wind howled, whispering tides of time that promised both enlightenment and peril. The moment was at hand; his choice would weave into the very fabric of his destiny, forever tethered to the ancient secrets hidden within the city's breath.

Unbeknownst to him, that choice loomed over the horizon like a gathering storm. Would the Sirocco blow him toward clarity, or would it sweep him into the abyss of forgotten histories? The shifting sands of time had always been fickle, and Karim stood at the eye of the tempest, ready to plunge deeper into the labyrinth of fate.

***

7
Shadows of Forgotten Figures

The air itself seemed to glimmer with echoes of the past as Karim strolled through the Medina, a mystery just waiting to be solved. Shadows flitted beyond the narrow alleyways, hints of figures he could not quite grasp, yet felt profoundly connected to. In those fleeting moments that pulled him from reality, he began to see the faces of his ancestors flickering in the corners of his vision, beckoning him to delve deeper into the fabric of his past.

Every turn he took felt orchestrated, as though some unseen hand, a force beyond the comprehension of mortal minds, guided him along forgotten routes that had long since been swallowed by the bustling life of the Medina. The scent of jasmine hung heavily in the air, intertwining with the aromas of spices that wafted from nearby souks, each breath an echo of tales whispered by souls long departed. With each step, he sensed a convergence happening, the essence of those who once walked these streets merging with his own hesitant presence.

As he paused by the ancient fountain, the water's surface rising and falling like the very breaths of those gone by, flashes of memory ignited within him. Stray lines of Sufi poetry he had once translated swept into his thoughts, illuminating the meaning behind the vibrations in the air. He closed his eyes, feeling the pulse of the Medina as if it were his own heartbeat, realising the endless dance of time: it was he who had stepped into their world, not them who had departed.

The feel of the stones beneath his fingertips sent more visions coursing through him. He could almost hear laughter, see the flickering back of a shawl as it flowed through the marketplace like a river of silk. But deeper undercurrents flowed beneath these shimmering glimpses. With every fleeting image, Karim sensed a growing urgency, a palpable tension. Whispers turned to shouts of warnings from the shadows: None would simply hover between realms without consequences.

As dusk began to blanket the Medina, a chill crept over him. The figures that had been gentle spectres started to twist and contort, revealing truths. Truths about his own lineage, about the forgotten history of the Medina, which he was perhaps not ready to confront. The streets seemed to squirm with purpose, and the gentle echoes morphed into clamours of forgotten stories, weighing heavily upon his shoulders. He stumbled over cobblestones, the world shifting unpredictably around him, leaving a cold dread in his gut. A realisation that following these glimpses might pull him deeper into the labyrinth of past sorrows.

Images of faces grew bolder and more defined, shadows growing menacing as they reached into his consciousness. He felt their presence pressing against his chest, collapsing the air around him. Karim hesitated, caught between the visceral pulse of history unfolding and the pulsating drive to break free while still clinging to their whispered revelations. The threads of fate intertwined, urging him to choose. A choice that carried the weight of his entire journey. To dive deeper into the abyss of memory, or to find refuge in the mundane reality of the modern day.

Suddenly, a voice broke through the din. A familiar voice that echoed with kindness and caution. Karim, it was urged, the map is incomplete; do not traverse paths that are too twisted. Know when to listen, and when to leave the past be. It was Selma, her presence merging with the night, illuminating the turmoil with a soft glow. Yet, uncertainty gnawed at him. Would he heed her warnings, or would he follow the trail of glimpse after glimpse across time, irrespective of the storm brewing in the threads that bound him to truth?

As shadows enveloped him, Karim took a deep breath, feeling the city's energy. Alive, restless, and enticing. The winds shifted, propelling him toward a confrontation with forces that would force him to decide: whether to yield to the ancestral call of his lineage and keep delving into the folds of history or retreat into an ordinary existence marked only by the functional realities of the modern world.

***

Karim felt the vibrations of the Medina underfoot, the subtle changes in the cobblestones as though they were alive, shifting to guide him deeper into the labyrinth. Each step resonated with an echo from the past, whispering through the narrow alleyways. He paused at a corner, heart racing, feeling the presence of those who had walked these paths long before, their energy melding into the dusty air around him.

As he ventured further, Karim's mind drifted to the stories he had uncovered through Horn's fragmented notes. What if the threads of fate he sought to map were woven by these very footsteps? The scent of jasmine wafted through the air, intoxicating and reminiscent of Selma's cryptic advice about attuning to the city's breath. Could it be that he was near some pivotal junction, a point where lines of time converged?

Turning right down yet another alley, a flicker of movement caught his eye. It was just a shadow, but it seemed too defined, too intentional to be merely the play of light. The figure appeared to linger just outside his vision, leading him onward. His anxiety mingled with a curious excitement; he felt compelled to follow, as if these steps might lead him closer to the truths he yearned to unveil.

The sensation of being observed washed over him, a subtle weight pushing against the back of his neck. He recalled Selma's words about the maps that chart territories from which one cannot return. Karim shook off the thought, pressing forward, his resolve strengthened by visions of Dr. Horn's journey. The air grew thicker around him, the whispers growing louder, entangling him in threads spun from long-forgotten tales.

He emerged into a small courtyard, hidden behind towering walls draped with vines, where the sun-drenched stones bore witness to innumerable secrets. In the centre stood a weathered fountain, its waters cascading softly. Approaching it, he could almost sense the soothing hum of ancestral voices lapping against the edges of his consciousness. He kneeled, dipping his fingers into the cool water, feeling an inexplicable connection, as if the fountain itself recognised him, acknowledging his quest.

Suddenly, the surrounding shadows shifted, and the presence he had felt before solidified into a tangible form. A ghostly figure in tradiional attire. Karim gasped, almost retreating, half convinced he was witnessing an apparition. The figure nodded slightly, its gaze urging him deeper into his own exploration. Karim trembled, torn between fear and the pull of destiny.

Time warped, seconds stretching into eternal moments, and Karim was struck by an overwhelming realisation. This was it. His past was beckoning him to confront the shadows, to pierce through the veil that separated memory from reality. Yet, the whispers warned him, shadows and light intertwined, enticing him with the allure of knowledge but threatening a descent into madness.

As the figure continued to fade, Karim felt a surge of urgency. He stood, his heart pounding, and the courtyard grew darker, the air heavy with anticipation. The footsteps around him seemed to pulse in rhythm with his heartbeat, each one landing like a question: would he follow, or would he retreat? The echoes of countless lives whispered promises of revelation. Still, they also carried the weight of consequences that seeped into the very stones beneath him.

With resolve flooding through him, Karim turned to retrace his steps, the knowledge that some doors, once opened, could never be closed echoing loudly in his mind. He knew he needed to grasp the strings of fate that lay just beyond the veil. Still, as the shadows deepened, he could feel *The Labyrinth* tightening around him, a reminder that every choice bore the potential for both knowledge and peril.

As Karim strolled deeper into the winding alleys of the Medina, an uncanny sense of resonance filled the air, reminiscent of whispers carried on the breeze. The sun dipped lower, casting elongated shadows that danced along the cobblestones, and he felt an invisible thread tugging at his awareness, reminding him of the stories buried in this labyrinth. Each turn of the corner led him closer to echoes of the past, an invitation intertwined with his present.

He paused near an ancient fountain, its surfaces worn smooth by time, the water trickling in a steady rhythm that felt like a heartbeat of the city itself. Leaning against the cold stone, he closed his eyes, allowing the sounds to envelop him. Suddenly, he heard the distant murmur of voices speaking in dialects long forgotten, and he felt the weight of their presence. Figures cloaked in the garb of bygone eras, weaving through the fabric of his reality.

Intrigued, Karim traced his fingers over the engraved markings on the fountain's edge, deciphering the faint inscriptions that hinted at lost narratives and unclaimed destinies. These marks weren't mere ornamentations; they felt alive, as if each carving held a memory aching to be recognised. Could they reveal the hidden paths Horn had posited? He felt a pulse of determination surge within him, his resolve edging closer to obsession with each new discovery.

As dusk descended upon the Medina, the atmosphere thickened with enchantment, and shadows morphed into spectral forms. He sensed a convergence, a simultaneous existence of past and present, urging him to delve deeper into the city's secrets. Following the intangible leads of scents, spices and the salty tang of the sea, Karim ventured further, where the streets writhed like serpents, whispering promises of enlightenment, yet carrying the weight of danger.

He recalled Selma's words about listening to the city's breath, realising that it was not only external voices he heard, but also an internal dialogue propelling him towards enlightenment or peril. The soft brush of an evening breeze caressed his face, and at that moment, he glimpsed another figure. This fleeting apparition mirrored his own silhouette, yet was dressed in traditional garments of another time.

Karim's heart raced. He caught the shadow's gaze before it vanished into the darkness, and he felt a connection, a thread binding him not just to the past but inviting him into its labyrinthine depths. The realisation struck him: the signs of another era weren't merely around him; they were intertwined with his essence. He took a deep breath, steeling himself for the journey ahead, knowing that every decision would ripple through the delicate fabric of history and memory.

His resolve ignited, Karim stepped forward, embracing the potential thrill of the unknown. With each footfall echoing through the Medina, he couldn't shake the idea that he wasn't just uncovering history; he was becoming part of it. But the question lingered—what truths awaited him in the shadows? And at what cost would he unearth them?

8
The Art of Obsession

Karim's obsession with Dr. Horn's work buried deeper into his daily life, suffocating whatever semblance of routine he had once clung to. The stacks of translations piled high on his desk served as delicate monuments to hours spent poring over fragmented texts. At the same time, the outside world faded into an indistinct hum. Faces of friends and acquaintances at the agency blurred, their concerns dismissed as mere echoes in the recesses of his mind. One afternoon, a stifling heat enveloped Tunis, the air thick with the scent of jasmine and the distant sound of salt. Yet, the sun's unforgiving glare could not illuminate the shadows encroaching upon his life.

He had neglected the simplest of duties, letting letters remain unanswered, allowing the plants on his balcony to wither in the relentless sun. The faint sounds of the bustling Halfaouine district slipped past his window unheeded. He no longer heard the laughter of children playing; all that surrounded him was Horn's haunting legacy and the fragmented whispers of the Anemoi.

One evening, as dusk draped its velvet fabric over the city, Karim returned to his work table, the once-inviting glow of a single lamp illuminating his cluttered chaos. He traced his fingers over Horn's diagrams, feeling the complex lines vibrate with energy, almost as if they pulsated with their own heartbeat. The excitement clawed at him, drawing him back into the labyrinth of Horn's metaphysical mapping. Each discovery increased his fervour, yet in that intensity lay the seeds of neglect, where personal engagement and responsibilities withered.

His passion consumed him like a fire raging unchecked, and even as he delved deeper, alerts in the corners of his consciousness grew louder. Memories of transient relationships, obligations to his work, and whispers of a life outside the confines of his flat. Karim's heart raced with the tantalising thrill of discovery, pushing aside guilt and the detached concern of others; they could wait. Then came the dream, vivid and unnerving, where he encountered Horn amidst an endless maze of shifting walls and swirling winds.

"You tread upon winds not meant for you," Horn warned, his voice echoing through the dreamscape, losing substance with each reverberation. "You might find what you seek, but at what cost?"

Karim jolted awake, drenched in sweat, Horn's haunting figure lingering in his thoughts. It was then that he realised his neglect had consequences he had yet to reckon with. The letters left unanswered had led to misunderstandings, the plants on his balcony had died, and the laughter of children playing had turned into distant echoes. These were the material-ising consequences of his obsession, like whis-pered warnings riding on the evening breeze.

As he plunged further into the depths of Horn's knowledge, his obsession took shape like the very winds he endeavoured to map. The air grew thick with tension, suffocated by his solitary pursuit; life was moving without him, a tide rising steadily while he drifted. Karim knew that to continue this way meant aban-doning the very essence of his humanity. Yet, each fleeting glimpse of understanding lured him deeper into the shadows of his own mak-ing, draining him of his vitality and leaving him a mere shell of his former self.

He shuddered at the thought of what might happen if he fully committed to the winds Horn spoke of. Was it a pathway to greatness, or an abyss shrouded in illusion? The precarious nature of his exploration gnawed at him, and he began to question whether his discover-ies would lead to enlightenment or madness. The uncertainty washed over him like a distant storm rolling in from the Mediterranean, and he felt the weight of his choices pressing down on him.

Karim's heart raced as he once again traced the curves of Horn's maps, but now the air around him seemed charged, vibrant with impending choice. The paradox loomed, bright and haunting. Would he chase the whisper of the winds, following Horn's path into the depths of knowledge, risking the life he had so carelessly forsaken? Or would he finally churn through the noise, breaking away to reclaim the ties to the world waiting just outside his door? The tension crackled in the air, ready to erupt; he was at a crossroads, and the weight of his choices was palpable, drawing the reader into the gravity of his situation.

Karim sat cross-legged on the faded Persian rug in his flat, papers strewn around him like fallen leaves, each one a fragment of Horn's theories and his own scattered thoughts. The scent of jasmine wafted in through the open window, mingling with the stale air of neglect. His fingers traced the intricate lines of one of Horn's maps, each curve a reminder of the mysteries that had consumed him. The world outside pulsed with life, but at this moment, he felt more alive than he ever had, his heartbeat syncing with the currents of possibility that swirled around him. His emotional journey was palpable, drawing the reader into his inner turmoil.

Each time he ventured into the Medina, he found himself seeing the familiar streets in a new light. The alleys, once mere pathways through a bustling market, now spoke to him, whispered secrets buried in every stone. Old men leaned against walls, their shadows long in the afternoon sun, as if waiting for an echo from the past. Karim jotted down notes in his worn notebook, his obsession guiding him through the city's labyrinth.

With newfound fervour, he began to sketch his own 'Anemoi Map,' not just an illustration of routes and locations but a vivid tapestry woven from his emotional experiences, the scents that filled his nostrils, and the fleeting glances of figures from another time. Each marker became a story, a convergence of whispers he hoped to decode. It was no longer about the destinations; it was about the sensations, the pulse of the city's breath beneath his fingertips, each mark on the paper a potent reminder that he was both mapping and being mapped by forces beyond his comprehension. The allure of his discoveries was undeniable, drawing the reader into his quest for understanding.

As twilight descended, Karim felt a shift in the air, an electric promise dancing on the horizon.

The shadows of the Medina grew deeper, and he wondered if he should capture the ethereal essence of dusk on his map. Would Horn have felt it too at this hour? Could such a thing as convergence be real, or was it merely the ramblings of a lonely scholar gone mad? His heart raced as he recalled Selma's words about maps that chart territories from which one cannot return. An involuntary shiver ran down his spine; what was he inviting upon himself?

With the experience of a new moon casting its faintest light across the Lake of Tunis, Karim felt the urgency to finalise his work. Each ink stroke was fraught with tension, a dance with the unknown, yet he yearned to embrace it. A potent mix of fear and exhilaration began to coil within him, surpassing the mundane rhythms of his life. He had begun to engage with the metaphysical winds; each gust beckoned him forward while warning him of the abyss that lay just beyond the threshold of understanding.

But as he placed the final touches on his map, a strange wind rattled the windowpanes. A sound now familiar yet unsettling. It glided through the streets of the Medina, echoing with voices that pressed into his consciousness. Suddenly, he was no longer alone. He could feel Horn's presence encroaching upon his reality, as if the very air he breathed was saturated with the echoes of his predecessor's obsession.

Karim's hand trembled slightly as he completed the last line on the parchment; the juxtaposition of clarity and chaos fused within him. The choice loomed larger than before: to follow the path he had illuminated or to retreat, accepting that some maps do not lead to the known but guide one into uncharted waters. He drew a deep breath, a silent resolve igniting within him, and the world around him snapped into focus. What awaited him in the labyrinth? The answer hung like the storm clouds gathering over La Marsa, waiting to unleash their hidden tempest.

***

The days turned into weeks as Karim plunged himself deeper into Horn's work, the elusive connections between maps, memory, and identity entwining themselves around his consciousness like ivy over ancient stone. He felt the pulsating rhythm of the city beneath his feet and in the fluttering pages of the notes. A synchrony echoing the metaphysical winds Horn had proposed. Each day, he neglected his duties at the cultural agency, and his colleagues grew increasingly concerned. Still, he couldn't

pull himself away from the allure of the unknown.

It was one afternoon, while the sun dipped low over the Medina, that the thrill of discovery struck him with a sudden jolt. Sitting at a small, weathered table in a café facing the bustling square, he sketched the outlines of his own personal Anemoi Map on an old parchment. As he placed the pen to paper, images of the labyrinthine streets, the whispers of jasmine in the souk, and the silhouettes of sun-bleached buildings melded into one another. With each stroke, he felt the map change. An ephemeral living entity shaped by his thoughts, emotions, and the very essence of the city itself.

Breathless with exhilaration, he stood abruptly, the chair scraping against the cobble-stones. The people around him blurred into the background, and he found himself drawn to the souk EL-Attarine. The perfume market. It was a site marked on Horn's fragmented diagrams, a location where he believed the metaphysical winds converged. The air was thick with tan-talising scents of spices, fragrant oils, and the earthiness of the Medina. Karim's heart raced. What would he discover here? What truths might the soft whispers of bygone poets reveal?

As he wandered through the alleys, he felt uncanny sensations wash over him. A feeling that time itself was oscillating, bending and twisting. It struck him that he had been here before in a dream, where shadows danced along the street corners. His fingers grazed the cooling stone walls, and a feeling of déjà vu surged. Voices drifted to him. Echoes of verses he had long translated, intertwined with the rustle of traders and patrons who moved as if choreographed by a silent conductor.

He paused before a stall draped with colourful textiles, his attention caught by an ancient astrolabe glinting under the soft glow of the setting sun. The vendor, a gaunt man with a tangled beard, noticed his lingering gaze and smiled knowingly. Ah, seeker of paths. This astrolabe measures more than just the stars; it whispers the truth of the winds. Karim's pulse quickened. Selma's astrolabe and its cryptic symbolism flashed in his mind. What if this were another piece of Horn's puzzle?

He purchased the device, cradling it carefully as he navigated back through the twisting streets. Excitement coursed through him like the currents of the Sirocco wind he had come to now associate with moments of clarity and confusion. Tonight was the night when the lunar phase would align with Horn's calculations from his notes. A convergence of mystic energies that could reveal profound insights or plunge him into the depths of madness.

Back in his flat, shadows danced on the walls

as the last light faded. The air felt electric, charged with possibility. He spread the notes and map before him, melding them with Horn's fragmented thoughts and his newfound astrolabe. Understanding hovered just beyond his reach, an intricate illusion crafted by his own obsession. As he searched for coherence in the chaos before him, he felt a burgeoning doubt. What if the more he discovered, the further he strayed from reality?

As the hour grew late, a restless energy wrapped around him, thrumming like the steady beat of a drum, heralding a moment of truth. Karim's fingers tightened around the astrolabe, the thrill of discovery pulsating through his veins. What lay on the other side of knowledge? With a silent breath, he prepared to follow the map he had created, stepping forward into the unknown, unaware that the veils of reality were poised to unfurl around him in ways he could scarcely imagine.

***

9
Reality's Mirage

Karim stood at the edge of Sidi Bou Said, his heart racing as he took in the scene before him. The village, painted in soft pastel hues of blue and white, glittered under the late afternoon sun like an ethereal vision lifted from a dream. He had long been captivated by this place, drawn by its postcard-perfect beauty. Yet, an unsettling feeling lingered in the depths of his mind. Was it truly as perfect as it appeared, or merely a façade, concealing something far more complex beneath its polished surface? The allure of Sidi Bou Said was undeniable, a siren's call that both tempted and tormented him.

The azure sky stretched infinitely above him, the sunlight casting playful shadows on the streets lined with Bougainvillea. The air was fragrant with the sweet scent of jasmine, yet within that intoxicating aroma, he sensed a bitterness, like the hint of salt on his tongue before a wave crashes against the shore. This idyllic village, which seemed to breathe charm and tranquillity, bubbled beneath with a different, darker energy that beckoned him to delve deeper.

As he wandered through the narrow alleys, Karim was aware of the subtle shifts in atmosphere, echoing the very essence of Horn's theories. The beauty of Sidi Bou Said felt like a mirage, enticing him closer while pulling him further away from the reality he knew. Despite the laughter of tourists and the vibrant chatter wafting through the streets, Karim felt a deep sense of isolation, like an outsider gazing through the looking glass of a different existence. He found himself questioning the authenticity of this picturesque village: was it a sanctuary of serenity, or a carefully constructed illusion masking the chaos and complexity of human experience?

His thoughts spiralled, considering how perception warped the narrative of truth in his experience. Here, in this seemingly perfect haven, he felt the weight of expectation. Both from himself and from those around him. The enchanting beauty of Sidi Bou Said seemed to mock his contemplations, presenting itself as a flawless jewel while whispering secrets that eluded his grasp. What was it that lingered just beyond the veil of this entrancing spectacle? What lay hidden beneath the layers of beauty that wrapped around the village like an impenetrable shroud?

As he paused by a small café overlooking the bay, the tranquillity of the waves rippling below clashed with the turbulence within him. The reflections danced across the water, swirling like the myriad thoughts tumbling unbidden in his mind. It was then that he felt it. A fleeting presence, a shadow just at the edge of his perception. He turned, heart pounding, but found only space. This feeling of being watched, observed by some unseen force, sent a chill down his spine. What truths lie entangled in these deceptive beauties? Was it possible that Sidi Bou Said harboured connections to Horn's disappearance, each flower hiding a whisper, each sweet scent a sign of something much more sinister?

The sky began to darken, the vivid colours of sunset bleeding into the horizon. Karim's heart raced; time was slipping through his fingers like grains of sand. He needed answers to push back against the mirage that enveloped him. At that moment, standing amidst the beauty that felt more like a prison than a paradise, he made a choice. He would delve beneath the surface, cutting through the seductive layers to reveal the truth lurking in the shadows. But deep down, he wondered. Was he prepared for whatever reality awaited him, or would he, too, become lost to the deceptive allure of Sidi Bou Said?

Karim stood at the edge of Sidi Bou Said,

the azure sea shimmering like a whispered promise, yet he felt a disquietude tugging at the corners of his mind. The village glimmered with an ethereal beauty, its whitewashed walls and cobalt doors stealing glimpses of lives lived in perfect harmony. The beauty of Sidi Bou Said was enchanting, a mystery that beckoned him to unravel its secrets. Yet, beneath the surface, he sensed an unsettling duality. A dissonance between what the town appeared to be and what it might conceal. In this picturesque trap, Karim felt both enchanted and ensnared.

He had come here to seek clarity, yet the clarity he found seemed refracted through a lens of uncertainty. As he wandered the narrow alleyways, shadows flickered at the periphery of his vision, whispering of past moments and lost truths. Each turn of the winding cobblestone path led him deeper into a kaleidoscope of shifting perceptions, where reality folded in upon itself like the layers of an intricate tapestry. He recalled Selma bin Hazm's riddles about the City's breath. He felt the pulsing rhythms around him resonate with the poetry he cherished. How much of what he perceived was real? And how much was crafted from the delicate threads of longing and fear?

The wind shifted, carrying with it a sense of foreboding, as if the ghosts of deep-seated memories stirred within the depths of his consciousness. With each inhalation, he felt the narrative of his existence swirling. A tempest of thought and feeling. Karim understood that perception was not a passive act; it was the very sculptor of truth, shaping and reshaping the narrative of his life. Like Horn's cryptic diagrams, his own life had become a map, with lines blurring between reality and illusion. What if, amidst the beauty of this picturesque haven, hidden truths lay waiting, perceptible only to those willing to traverse beyond the façade?

With an urgent pull, he found himself at the edge of the cliff, where the sea met the sky in a breathless embrace. The waves crashed relentlessly, relentless metaphors of a world both alive and indifferent. Karim closed his eyes, surrendering to the cacophony of nature and the intertwining of past and present. Suddenly, he glimpsed a fleeting figure, a woman draped in the whispers of time. A ghost adorned in shadow and memory, beckoning him to unlock the secrets buried within the very fabric of perception itself. A deep rumble echoed through him as he opened his eyes, realising that clarity might demand a price, colliding with the very heart of reality's mirage.

As the evening sun dipped lower, casting long shadows across Sidi Bou Said, he felt a tremor of fear intertwine with exhilaration. Was he veering toward enlightenment, or could he potentially lose himself, consumed by the labyrinth he was navigating? Karim recognised that each insight gained could also unravel the very tapestry he sought to understand, bringing a deeper challenge. An invitation from knowledge that held whispers of madness, urging him to confront the elusive boundary between what he thought he understood and what lay beyond his comprehension. With resolve ignited in his chest, he stepped forward, knowing that he stood on the precipice of discovery, ready to face whatever awaited beyond the surface of elegant deception.

***

Karim leaned against the cool, weathered stone of Sidi Bou Said's balustrade, surveying the glittering Mediterranean below. The village's azure and white façades dazzled under the midday sun. Yet, an unsettling thought gnawed at him. Was this beauty merely a carefully constructed façade? As the wind tossed his thoughts between the whispers of poetry and the scattered notes of Dr. Horn, he felt the weight of his quest pressing down like the oppressive heat of the day.

It was one thing to uncover forgotten truths hidden within Horn's papers, but the journey demanded more than his intellectual curiosity; it strained his very reality. Each day spent decoding the fragments felt like another thread woven into a tapestry he couldn't quite grasp. The allure of knowledge shimmered like the sea, beckoning him closer. Yet, he understood. What lay beneath its surface might be far more treacherous than he imagined.

Karim's fingers brushed against the aged parchment in his satchel, the meticulously translated lines a testament to his dedication. Yet as he watched tourists traverse the narrow streets, laughing and snapping photographs of the idyllic scenery, he felt increasingly isolated. Where they sought pleasures of sight and sound, he yearned for more profound wisdom, yet the more he sought the truth in his research, the more he lost something essential: the connection to the world around him.

As shadows stretched and the sun dipped lower, casting golden hues across the village, he recalled Selma's words in her cryptic manner. "Some maps chart territories from which one cannot return," she had said, her voice a soft breeze through the cluttered antiques of her shop. It echoed ominously in his mind, a warning that was inextricably intertwined with his obsession. Was he perhaps standing at the precipice of a truth too perilous for anyone to accept? With each whispered secret he unearthed, Karim questioned if he was unearthing the fabric of the universe or merely unravelling his sanity.

A familiar scent of jasmine wrapped around him, momentarily grounding his spiralling thoughts. As he turned to the source, a sudden gust of wind rustled the branches overhead, carrying with it an ethereal melody that seemed to beckon him further into the depths of uncertainty. He began to wonder if he was a mere interpreter of Horn's theories, or if he risked becoming a participant in the very metaphysical game he sought to understand.

Determined to push through the encroaching doubts, Karim made his way down the winding paths of Sidi Bou Said, feeling as if each step took him deeper into the labyrinthine maze that mirrored the complexity of his inquiries. The world around him transformed; the vibrant blue and white buildings murmured secrets, implying that reality itself was as fluid as the shifting sands of the Medina.

As he approached a secluded spot overlooking the sea, he stopped short, the weight of impending decisions palpable in the air. He could feel it. The nexus of knowledge and peril, teetering on the edge of revelation. Every shred of insight he sought threatened to plunge him into a void of uncertainty. Karim had come to realise that the pursuit of knowledge wasn't merely an act of enlightenment, but could very well be the catalyst for his undoing.

As dusk began to envelop the village, casting shadows across the landscape, Karim sensed that he stood on a threshold. The shimmering illusion of Sidi Bou Said was alluring. Yet, the deeper truths it concealed could bind him in an inescapable labyrinth from which there was no return. Would pursuing the full breadth of Horn's theories lead him to clarity, or was this picturesque mirage merely an entrapment designed to ensnare the curious minds who dared to challenge it?

With his heart racing and mind reeling, he took a deep breath, confronting the daunting reality that the path forward promised not only revelation but significant cost. As if sensing his internal struggle, the wind intensified for a moment, swirling around him before dissipating into the evening air, leaving behind a profound silence. In that instant, it became all too clear—this was not merely a quest for knowledge, but a reckoning with the very essence of reality itself, a delicate dance on a precipice that might forever alter the fabric of his existence.

10
The Nexus of Knowledge

When Karim walked through the grand entrance of the Zitouna Mosque Library, he could feel the weight of many years pressing down on him. The air was thick with the scent of ageing parchment and the hushed whispers of countless scholars who had traversed these vast chambers. Marble columns soared towards the elaborate ceiling, their intricate designs swirling like the thoughts that raced through his mind. Here, in this sacred space, he could sense the intersection of knowledge and faith, a place where the past bled into the present.

Each shelf was a testament to the labyrinthine nature of human thought, containing tomes that spanned disciplines, from philosophy to astronomy, poetry to mysticism. Karim's fingers brushed against their spines as he navigated the narrow aisles, drawn to the hidden corners that seemed to hold secrets waiting to be uncovered. Among the scrolls, he discovered a series of mismatched texts, their fragile paper carrying the weight of forgotten lore and dangerous truths. The librarian, an elderly figure wrapped in the traditional garb of a scholar, watched him with piercing eyes that seemed to judge his intentions, adding to the allure of the forbidden knowledge.

As he delved deeper, Karim unearthed a collection of writings that hinted at the metaphysical winds Horn had theorised about. Enigmatic maps annotated with strange symbols and esoteric references. They spoke of paths not taken, of choices that would ripple through time like the flow of air across the Medina. The urgency of his quest pressed down on him like the humid Tunisian air, and every passing moment heightened the thrill of discovery, intertwining his fate with the ghosts of the past.

In one dimly lit corner, he stumbled upon a manuscript that sent a shiver down his spine. The text was both familiar and foreign, echoing the piercing voice of Selma bin Hazm from their previous encounters. It warned of the cost of seeking forbidden knowledge, of maps that could lead one to the abyss. The realisation dawned on him that each page turned could bring him closer to understanding Horn's destiny, or push him into a realm he could never return from. His heart raced as the implications unravelled in his mind, the tension mounting as he grasped the delicate balance between enlightenment and the looming danger of madness.

Karim's pulse quickened as he considered the choice before him, the library an ever-closing labyrinth in which knowledge became a double-edged sword. In this nexus of knowledge, he could either illuminate the darkness surrounding Horn's disappearance or plunge into obscurity, forever chasing phantoms. As the sun dipped lower in the sky, casting long shadows across the marble floor, the air trembled with unspoken promises and foreboding echoes of what lay ahead.

As Karim stepped into the Zitouna Mosque Library, the air hummed with a weight that was more than the ancient texts lining the shelves. Each tome exuded an aura of secrets, whispers of forbidden knowledge that echoed between the cracked walls, reminding him of the thin veil between enlightenment and madness. The library, a sanctuary of the written word and thought, seemed alive with the pulse of history, drawing him closer to the texts that murmured with both allure and danger.

He ventured deeper, threading his fingers across the spines of manuscripts, each touch igniting a flicker of apprehension. Among the dust and shadows, he discovered a covered table, upon which lay a collection of scrolls, bound in fraying twine and waxen seals. They were labelled in a script that danced with an eerie elegance, luring him into the tumultuous waters of knowledge he had spent years cautiously navigating. It was as if these texts knew his name, knew the depths of his curiosity, and dared him to unearth their truths.

Petals of jasmine lingered in the air, a scent that had become entwined in his pursuits. Yet, this time, the fragrance conjured a sense of foreboding, hinting at the labyrinthine paths knowledge could take. As he unfurled a scroll, letters leapt to life, revealing theories that intertwined reality and illusion with a complexity he had yearned for yet now regarded with trepidation. The revelations hinted at the Nexus of Knowledge. A convergence of truths that could alter the essence of existence itself.

Among these fragments, Karim came upon a reference to Horn. A name that stirred dark echoes within him. It spoke of forbidden practices and dangerous truths locked away from the eyes of the unworthy, suggesting that some knowledge was not meant to be unearthed. The audacity of these assertions ignited a flicker of rebellion in his chest. Could he, an ordinary translator on the fringes of academic respectability, truly grasp this arcane wisdom? The thought filled him with a heady mix of thrill and despair.

The shadows danced longer as night crept silently upon the library's sacred space. As the final rays of dusk faded from outside, the words before him seemed to shimmer uneasily, coalescing into images of the labyrinthine Medina that had both ensnared and liberated him. Each phrase unfurled, a beckoning to explore the boundaries of existence, yet within the urgency of enlightenment lay a chasm of peril. He sensed it. Knowledge with the power to unravel accepted reality, a truth so profound it could consume him whole, yet also the promise of enlightenment and understanding.

Karim's heart raced. The very air around him thickened as clarity and chaos danced on the edges of his consciousness. He dared to summon Horn's ghost, whispering into the disarray of worlds that existed just beyond his perception. Driven by a compulsion deeper than mere curiosity, should he cross the threshold into forbidden texts and embrace the dangerous truths? Would he emerge enlightened, or be swallowed by the darkness that lingered at the fringes of knowledge?

With trembling hands, he turned the pages, images swirling before his mind's eye, conflicting memories and desires merging into one precipice of revelation. The libidinous pursuit of knowledge led him toward the precipice. This treacherous void promised clarity but threatened to plunge him into despair. How far was he willing to journey through this nexus, and at what cost?

***

As Karim stepped through the ancient archway of the Zitouna Mosque Library, he felt a palpable shift in the atmosphere, the weight of centuries pressing against him. Rows of weathered tomes surrounded him, their spines cracked and dusty, sheltering secrets whispered in the hushed reverence of the past. Each title was an invocation, a key to infinite doors of thought. Yet, he could not shake the sensation that some of these doors were best left unopened.

He wandered deeper into the library's heart, where the sunlight fractured through intricate latticework, casting a mosaic of illumination upon the weathered pages. The air was heavy with the scent of ageing paper, mingled with the faint aroma of incense. Here, the boundaries between the reader and the text blurred into obscurity, as if the words themselves were alive, waiting to be spoken, to be understood. Yet, he felt a growing trepidation; certain volumes exuded a hum of danger, resonating with the unbridled curiosity that had driven him to this place.

Karim's fingers trembled as they brushed against the spines of forbidden texts—cautionary tales of knowledge that birthed madness, of scholars who lost themselves in labyrinthine complexities of their own making. In his heart, a conflict raged. To possess knowledge was to unlock potential, yet this path could lead to ruin. As he leafed through one particularly ornate manuscript, he recognised in its script the echoes of Horn's musings. The metaphysical winds, the Anemoi Mapping that beckoned him. The burden of this knowledge weighed heavily, pressing him to confront not just the potential it held, but the irrevocable change it could bring to his life.

At that moment of contemplation, a flicker across the periphery of his vision caught his attention. He turned, the library's shadows seemingly shifting. A curious figure lingered just beyond the stacks. The figure wore a long, flowing robe, its fabric reminiscent of the ancient texts surrounding them. Karim felt a rush of adrenaline, the urgency of instinct drawing him closer. Was this another seeker, or perhaps a wraith conjured from the pages he had turned? As he approached, the figure whispered, voice barely audible over the silence of the library: Are you prepared to bear the burden of what you seek?

The words hung like a fragile thread in the air, and the weight of them pressed upon

Karim's chest, momentarily stealing his breath. He opened his mouth to respond, yet doubt curdled within him, rendering him mute. The figure leaned in closer, its features obscured, as if mocking the clarity Karim so desperately sought. Knowledge is a vast repository, yes, but its depths can drown those who delve without caution. With a jarring twist, the figure melted into the shadows, leaving Karim alone to grapple with the implications of its eerie warning.

Heart racing, Karim returned to the manuscript, his gaze drawn inexorably to the inked diagrams mapping the winds of fate, streams of possibility converging on the very heart of Tunis. It felt as though an unseen force pressed against his back, urging him to discover whether he could navigate this labyrinth of knowledge without losing himself. The library morphed before him into a maze, each choice branching out into uncharted territories, threatening to fracture his sense of reality.

As he reached for the manuscript once more, the tremor in his hands became a storm within. He had entered the Nexus of Knowledge, yet the floodgates of understanding threatened to burst wide open, each word a potential dagger in his pursuit of truth. It was a tantalising dance on the edge of madness, and he felt the breath of the infinite repository wrap around him like a cold embrace, whispering not just of potential, but of dire consequence.

II
Convergence of Winds

Karim felt a sense of wakefulness inside him as the moon moved across the inky-black sky of Tunisia, giving the winding streets of the Medina a silvery tint. The gentle illumination seemed to breathe life into his surroundings, shifting shadows amidst the bustling market stalls. He remembered Dr. Horn's fragmented notes, which mentioned the convergence of winds and their connection to lunar cycles. A theme that now echoed through his consciousness, resonating with the patterns he had come to understand. This anticipation of what was to come added a layer of intrigue to his journey.

Karim stood at the edge of the fountain in the courtyard, recalling the scents of jasmine and spices wafting through the air. He could almost sense the pull of the moon, as if its gravitational embrace had woven strands of memory through the very fabric of time. Horn had suggested that these lunar phases were not merely celestial markers; they were moments of potential, where the energies of the Earth and sky met, creating bridges to uncharted realms and whispering secrets of fate.

A shadow shifted in the corner of his eye, prompting him to turn, yearning to trace the source. The figure, though indistinct, radiated an aura of familiarity as if it belonged to a dream long forgotten. It felt as if the phase of the moon were orchestrating a dance between past and present, and Karim, caught in its rhythm, approached. The deeper he delved into Horn's understanding of the lunar cycles, the more he felt tethered to something larger than himself, a cosmic synchronisation threatening to unravel the boundaries of his reality.

As twilight deepened, shadows lengthened around him, the eerie tranquillity sharpening into an acute tension that vibrated in the air. Karim realised that tonight was a convergence, one he had meticulously marked in Horn's notes. The air hummed with unspoken promises and fears, reminding him of Selma's cautionary words about maps that charted territories from which one cannot return. His heart raced as he absently traced the etchings on the worn paper, contemplating the choice laid bare before him: to fully engage with the unknown or retreat to the safety of his translated poems. The weight of his decision hung heavy in the air, making the gravity of his choices palpable to the readers.

Each tick of the clock resounded in his mind, amplifying the urgency of his next actions. The lunar glow above shifted, casting an ethereal light onto the cobblestones like a signpost of destiny. The world around him felt alive with possibility, shimmering at the edges like the mirage of Sidi Bou Said. What awaited him on the other side of this temporal threshold? Could he decode the convergence of Horn's theories and manifest the mythical Anemoi winds, or was he merely another seeker destined to lose himself in the labyrinth of the Medina? The allure of the unknown was palpable, fuelling his curiosity and eagerness to discover more.

As the moon reached its apex, he found strength in his resolve. The convergence was at hand, a moment suspended between breaths. A decision, a leap into a nebulous space where knowledge and madness conjoined. Karim stepped forward, his heart pounding like the distant drums that echoed from the souks, urging him to follow the winds and to embrace whatever lay beyond the veil of the present moment.

***

As the sun dipped beneath the horizon, casting a golden hue over the Medina, Karim stood at the edge of his small flat, contemplating the notes left behind by Dr. Horn. The air was thick with the scent of spices wafting from the nearby souks, and he felt the familiar pull of the city's labyrinthine streets, each twist and turn a potential revelation waiting to unfurl before him. Every fragment of Horn's writings seemed to dance in his mind, urging him to decode the mysteries interwoven within them.

Karim carefully spread out the fragments on his cluttered table, squinting at the scrawl of Horn's handwriting, dense with metaphors and the elusive promise of knowledge. The notion of 'Anemoi Mapping' beckoned like a riddle he needed to solve; it was a concept Horn had developed, a method of deciphering the intersection of winds and lunar phases. It was as if he could almost feel the winds of fate swirling through the pages, whispering secrets that remained tantalisingly unreachable. As he read a specific passage about the intersection of winds and lunar phases, the hair on the back of his neck prickled, igniting an electric urgency within him.

At that moment, the quiet of his flat felt suffocating. He needed to immerse himself in the physical reality of the Medina, to chase the echoes of Horn's thoughts through the very streets that had long concealed their own wisdom. Clutching the notes like a lifeline, he stepped out into the dusky streets, the shadows lengthening around him, alive with the distant sounds of laughter and the soft rustle of fabric in the evening breeze.

Karim navigated the winding alleys, his senses heightened. Each corner of the Medina unfolded new perspectives, familiar yet curiously altered, as if the city itself was responding to his presence. The streets whispered back at him; the laughter of children morphed into a distant echo of a Sufi verse he had translated long ago, calling him deeper into its folds. Could the very essence of the city be a reflection of Horn's theories? Was it possible that the winds themselves carried the weight of memories, guiding him toward the profound truths he yearned to uncover?

Before long, he found himself standing before a weathered fountain, its waters shimmering under the fading twilight. Horn's notes had highlighted this very spot, yet it felt charged with an energy beyond the physical. The water rippled, creating circular patterns that mirrored the complex diagrams in his mind. Karim leaned closer, drawing a breath that felt heavy with significance, as if the air itself had thickened, anticipating his next move.

With a sudden gust, the Sirocco wind stirred, a powerful and often unpredictable force in the region, sending a shiver down his spine. It seemed to beckon him, urging him to plunge into the unknown. The convergence Horn had spoken of felt imminent. A moment when the threads of fate and memory would weave into a tapestry of revelation. Yet, unease clutched at his heart as he considered the implications. Was he prepared to embrace whatever truths awaited him, or would the pursuit of this knowledge lead him into the very abyss Horn had warned against?

As darkness enveloped the Medina, an unsettling atmosphere crept in, as if the city itself were holding its breath. The flickering lanterns danced in the shadows, their light revealing fleeting figures in the periphery. Who were they? Karim's pulse quickened, and the city's heartbeat seemed to synchronise with his own. It was then that he realised that the winds of change were not merely metaphoric; they were manifestations of his own unfolding journey, and the path he treads was laden with echoes of his own past.

In that electrifying moment, the weight of his quest became crystal clear. He stood at the precipice of revelation, ready to unveil the enigmas that intertwined the fates of himself, Horn, and the very essence of the city. But as the winds of the Medina began to swirl with increasing intensity, Karim sensed the precarious nature of what lay ahead; enlightenment was woven with the threads of madness, and the unknown was a double-edged sword.

***

As the lunar phases shifted, Karim felt an electric pulse within him, as if the very fabric of knowledge was vibrating, beckoning him to weave a narrative from the fragmented threads of experience he had gathered. The convergence of winds that Horn had so obsessively outlined in his notes began to surface in Karim's mind like a phantom, alluring yet elusive. He sensed that the answers he sought lay not just in the texts and drawings strewn across Horn's villa, but within the shifting alleys of the Medina itself.

Karim closed his eyes and traced the lines of Horn's maps in the air with his fingertips, each curve reflecting a memory, a place, a fleeting thought. The city breathed around him as he delved deeper into the layers of perception, understanding that each moment in the Medina held the potential to unlock another piece of the puzzle. The scent of spices from the souks filtered through his window, filling him with a sense of nostalgia and urgency, as if each whiff twisted through time, ever-present yet always just beyond his grasp.

He set out once more, driven by an insatiable

need to connect these dots between Horn's whispering theories and his own experiences. The moment he stepped into the clamorous heart of the Medina, Karim felt the air shift, aware that he was being guided by unseen hands. Familiar street corners morphed, leading him to hidden staircases and long-forgotten fountains. Each step was rhythmic, synchronised with the muted echoes of the city. This heartbeat resonated with his own pulsating curiosity.

In his wanderings, he stopped at a small café, where the scent of roasted coffee mingled with the floral notes of jasmine in the air. There, he overheard a conversation between two men, their words reverberating with haunting familiarity. Phrases he had translated echoed back to him, stirring memories of solitude and poetic yearning. Karim grasped at these threads, each syllable becoming a connection, a bridge to understanding the metaphysical currents that Horn had struggled to define.

The sun dipped lower in the sky, casting a golden hue over the complex labyrinth of the Medina, as he approached Selma bin Hazm's antique shop. Every time he sought her wisdom, he found something different waiting for him. Secrets wrapped in riddles and artefacts whispering their own tales. Today, she was rearranging a collection of dusty astrolabes, her fingers dancing over their surfaces with a reverence that seemed to breathe life into the shop's stillness.

"Listen closely, Karim," Selma intoned, her voice a soft ember alight with meaning. "The city's breath reveals patterns, but it is up to you to interpret the signs. Maps can guide you to places, but only your heart can navigate the truth within."

Her eyes bore into his, compelling him to penetrate the layers of meaning that were constantly unfolding around him. The astrolabes, she explained, could measure the inclination of whispers. Yet, each one of them had its fault. A crack, perhaps mirroring the inherent imperfections of their knowledge.

Karim felt the weight of her words settle inside him. He left the shop with a renewed sense of purpose, pondering her metaphorical treasure. His heart raced as he recalled Horn's notes on the convergence, recognising that the time was imminent. The boundaries of his own understanding had begun to blur, challenging him to take risks he had never dared before. If he were indeed to search for Horn, he would have to embrace uncertainty, potentially navigating toward precipices that might lead him into realms beyond comprehension.

As dusk cloaked the Medina, Karim sought the fountain he had visited days before. Its water, silvered by the lunar glow, shimmering under the fading sunlight. This place, he felt, was integral to the convergence Horn spoke of. But as he arrived, a gust of wind stirred the water's surface, rippling outward in chaotic waves, reminiscent of the whirlwind of thoughts racing through his mind. Was he on the brink of revelation, or merely entangled in an illusion?

Karim leaned over the fountain, captivated by the fragments of a recall that danced just unreachable. The echoes of the past flooded in; images of Horn, stories of the winds, and the sharp clarity of a decision were all crystallising within him. As the moon climbed higher, its silvery light revealing the hidden contours of the city, he understood: it was not merely about connecting the dots of his journey, but embracing the ambiguous paths that led him to this pivotal moment.

12

The Decision Point

Karim stood by the window of his cramped flat, a solitary figure in a painting that longed for the strokes of a brush to bring it alive. The Halfaouine district bustled beneath him, yet he felt isolated, the weight of the world pressing down on him as twilight descended over Tunis. He held Horn's fragmented notes in trembling hands, the words dancing before his eyes like phantoms of the past. Each line resonated with urgency, the convergence of metaphysical winds creeping closer. Time slipped through his fingers like sand, and he felt the pressure of an unseen clock ticking behind him.

Completing the Anemoi Map, a complex and enigmatic creation, had become an obsession for Karim. It was a labyrinth of thoughts, each path winding tighter with each passing moment. He pored over his sketches and notes, desperate to make sense of the paths he had traced through the Medina. The essence of Horn's theories, which the map was meant to elucidate, felt like a siren's call, intoxicating yet laden with peril. What if he dared follow the currents he had charted on the map, only to find himself lost in the chaos of map and reality intertwining, each twist and turn leading him deeper into an abyss from which there was no return?

With each flicker of candlelight, memories of

his solitary existence gnawed at him. Would he risk everything — his reclusive life, his perceived reality — for a chance at understanding the deeper truths Horn hinted at? As the final threads of dusk wove into the fabric of the night, a whisper began to unfurl within him, a tension between fear and exhilaration that mirrored the city outside, where shadows loomed large and secrets lay in wait.

Yet doubt, insidious and persistent, crept into his consciousness. What awaited him at the threshold of this decision? Would the act of completing the map unveil enlightenment, or would he stumble into a labyrinthine nightmare from which neither he nor Horn could emerge? The choice felt almost primordial, and as he traced the elegant curves of the map, the ink revealed patterns that shimmered like glistening strands of fate. Every breath became heavier, each pulse a reminder that tomorrow might lead him into the unknown, into the convergence of metaphysical winds, a metaphor for the forces of fate and choice that were drawing him closer to a pivotal moment.

Just as he poised his pen over the final detail, a gust of wind gusted through the open window. The Sirocco, perhaps, bringing with it a haunting reminder of Selma's words: "Some maps chart territories from which one cannot return." Karim's heart raced, caught between the familiar comfort of his old ways and the daunting leap into enigmatic possibilities. A single decision stood before him, a crossroads that could forever alter the atlas of his existence and draw him closer to Horn's spectral fate or liberate him into an understanding beyond comprehension.

At that moment, with the weight of the map congealing into a singular firmament of purpose, he hesitated. The convergence of metaphysical winds was no longer a mere theory; it loomed like a spectre, its face hidden behind folds of uncertainty. Completing the map felt like crossing an unforgiving threshold. He wondered. Would this be the moment that illuminated all he had ever sought, or would it reveal a shadowed truth, dragging him into the depths where no light could penetrate?

As the sun dipped behind the horizon, casting a golden glow over the Medina, Karim's heart raced within his chest. He stood at the threshold of his decision, the weight of Horn's fragmented notes pressing heavily against his thoughts. Completing the Anemoi Map felt obsolete yet imperative, the convergence beckoning him with promises of knowledge mingled with madness. The whispers of wind through the cobbled streets seemed to echo visions from his dreams. Fragmented glimpses of forgotten figures, and timeless truths hidden in the folds of the city's fabric, serving as a reminder of the city's history and the secrets it held.

He could almost hear Selma's voice, a gentle warning threaded with riddles: "Some maps chart territories from which one cannot return." The scent of blooming jasmine wafted through the air, thick and intoxicating, as if inviting him deeper into the labyrinthine alleys. At that moment, he felt pulled, caught between allure and danger, each pulse of his heart urging him closer to the abyss that lay beyond the known.

The details of his creation unfolded before his mind's eye – the intertwining paths of fate depicted within his map, a living, breathing document that reflected not just geography, but also the gentle currents of memory and possibility. Thoughts of Horn flickered through his mind. Had the esteemed scholar vanished into this very void? Or had he found a higher truth within its depths?

Shadows lengthened on the walls as he traced a finger across the delicate parchment, floodgates of hesitation opening within him.

The final strokes would set him on a course from which there was no turning back. Karim's hands trembled as he held the compass pen, feeling the weight of consequence pressing against his resolve. Was he ready to plunge into the storm, to face the chaos of enlightenment?

Outside, the winds began to howl, echoing the turmoil inside him. The convergence they had whispered about in hushed tones was upon him, the very air charged with an electric possibility. Karim stepped back, his gaze locking with the deepening twilight that suffused the air with secrets. At that moment, one question rose starkly before him: what awaited him in the abyss. Illumination or irrevocable madness?

Resignation washed over him, entwined with fear. Perhaps the abyss was not something to be faced alone. With a shaky breath, Karim felt the encroaching darkness beneath each layer of his carefully constructed realities; the time had come to embrace these shadows. Would he retreat into safety, or would he dare to weave the threads of his existence within the unpredictable winds that twisted through the streets of Tunis?

As the last traces of daylight vanished, Karim found himself standing on the precipice, a lone figure poised between realms, the echo of the city's heartbeat resonating in his soul. He took in a deep breath, the air thick with history and possibility, and prepared to plunge into the uncertainty that awaited him. The choice, he realised, was no longer his alone to bear. The city's breath had become his own, and now, it beckoned him to step into the unknown.

***

As Karim stood before the diverse yet disarrayed fragments of his Anemoi Map, he could feel the pressure weighing down on him. A cacophony of emotions, fears, and unspoken desires surging forth like the very winds he sought to grasp. Here, in the sanctuary of his cluttered flat overlooking the vibrant Halfaouine district, he could no longer avoid the choice that loomed before him: to finalise the map and plunge into the depths of its revelations or to walk away, letting the weight of knowledge remain uncharted.

Outside, the Medina pulsed with life, the sound of merchants haggling and the aroma of spices intertwined with the scent of jasmine and sea salt. Yet, within him, an abyss echoed louder. Would the abyss offer enlightenment, or would it pull him into madness? Each choice lingered like a spectre. He envisioned Horn, perhaps on the cusp of some outrageous truth or lost among the metaphysical mazes he had sought to navigate, a brilliant mind shackled by the consequences of its pursuits.

Karim's thoughts spiralled as he pondered the ramifications of his decision. Following Horn's path could mean uncovering profound truths and revealing the darker corners of reality that had remained hidden. He could almost hear Selma's cryptic warnings about the nature of such maps, reminding him that each step taken without care could invite perilous consequences. Now, the choice before him felt like a delicate dance between the thrill of discovery and the heavy cloak of responsibility.

The depth of his commitment weighed on him, tight in his chest like the tightening grasp of the Sirocco wind that swept through La Marsa, unpredictable and relentless. His fingers trembled slightly, brushing over the paper, where the ink of Horn's thoughts pooled like the waters of the Lake of Tunis, dark and unfathomable. If he completed the map, would he become the architect of his destiny or just another fragile figure in Horn's story. A cautionary tale warning against the depths one can delve when mapping the intersections of fate?

Karim inhaled deeply, the familiar scents of coffee and old parchment offering him fleeting comfort amidst the tempest of uncertainty in his mind. The choice hung in the air, waiting for him to grasp it. The city outside beckoned as if it held the answers to his unasked questions, while the echoes of the past whispered secrets only he could translate. He could feel the pulse of Tunis, a confluence of his own fears and desires, leading him toward a clarity that felt both alluring and dangerous.

Just as his resolve began to crystallise, the shadows in the room shifted subtly, casting new illuminations on the fragile boundaries of his reality. Karim clenched his jaw, staring at the map, heart racing as the weight of every potential consequence. A whisper in time wrapped around his throat. In that fleeting moment, he felt the dizzying push of possibility, and he realised that the choice he would make was not simply about completing a map; it was about understanding who he was in the sprawling labyrinth of existence that unfolded before him.

With a deepened breath and fading hesitation, he reached for his pen, the ink poised as a conductor's baton, ready to ignite the symphony that awaited beyond this decision point. As he prepared to carve his destiny, the restless winds of change swept through his mind, entwining with his thoughts and unravelling in an intricate dance of fate, memory, and possibility. All those winds swirling towards the heart of

Tunis, propelling him into the unknown.

13
The Threshold of Reality

As Karim stood at the edge of the Lake of Tunis, its waters shimmering under the late afternoon sun, he felt a disquieting pull, as though reality itself was beckoning him to dive beneath its surface. The lake was a liminal space, a threshold between the known world of the bustling Medina and the vast unknown that lay beyond. He hesitated, a tight knot forming in his stomach; the possibility of stepping into the unknown was both exhilarating and terrifying, yet undeniably alluring.

The air was thick with the scent of sea salt and jasmine, intoxicating yet heavy with undertones of something deeper, something primal. Karim recalled Selma's words, her warnings about the city's breath and the maps that could lead one astray. The weight of her astrolabe in his mind was palpable, the flawed instrument that had always seemed to suggest that not all paths could safely be travelled. Was he prepared to navigate these uncharted waters where reality blurred with illusion?

The lake's surface danced in the wind, ripples distorting both light and reflection. Karim considered his journey thus far, the fragments of Horn's notes leading him to this very moment. Each encounter, the whispered verses of Sufi poetry, the riddles shared with Selma, the fleeting glimpses of historical figures in the Medina, had been a step towards unveiling a more encompassing truth. And yet, clarity felt elusive, like the shimmering surface that refused to show him its depths.

He took a step forward, his thoughts swirling like the currents in the lake. Each breath filled him with apprehension and the promise of discovery. What lay beneath the surface? Knowledge? Enlightenment? Or madness? As the shadows lengthened and twilight embraced the land, the lake transformed, its dark depths reflecting a world both familiar and foreign. The cosmos beyond the horizon intertwined with the consciousness within him. Karim could taste the potent possibility of what lay ahead, more thrilling than any poem he had ever translated. His struggle was real, his journey intense.

With one final glance at the familiar shores of the city, Karim plunged into the water. The coolness enveloped him, and he felt the exhilarating rush of being suspended between worlds. Silence closed around him, punctuated only by the distant echoes of his own heartbeat. As he sank deeper, the boundaries of logic began to dissolve, unravelling like the intricate patterns of Horn's bizarre maps, revealing a hidden complexity of intersections and decisions. Karim was not merely a passive observer; he was both creator and creation in this enigmatic space.

But just as soon as clarity emerged from the depths, a swift current attempted to pull him under. Memories flashed before him. Fragments of conversations, the rhythm of the city's breath, and a haunting question spun from Selma's riddle: "Some maps chart territories from which one cannot return." Would he find the knowledge he sought, or would he become ensnared in its entwining currents, lost forever?

As he fought against the pull of the deep, the tension of his choice outweighed every shred of confidence he had mustered. The realisation struck him: diving into this liminal space was not just an act of courage, but a confrontation with his own identity, beliefs, and fears. Turning back was a danger of its own, yet pressing forward invited unknown spirals of time, space, and consciousness that Horn had hinted at yet never fully revealed.

His lungs began to ache, but Karim pressed forward, determined to seek the heart of the lake's secret. As the water enveloped him, he felt the ancient whispers of knowledge ripple through him, urging him deeper into the unknown's embrace. What lay ahead remained uncertain, yet one thing was clear: the threshold of reality, a concept he had grappled with in his philosophical studies, was no longer a mere boundary but a transformative passage into something profoundly enigmatic.

***

As Karim stood at the water's edge, the pulsating surface of the Lake of Tunis seemed to bridge two worlds, whispering secrets that tantalised his senses. The twilight cast long shadows across the water, making the space feel both infinite and confining. He inhaled sharply, the scent of salt mixing with the dampness of the air, as if the lake itself were drawing breath with him. For him, this was the sanctuary where knowledge flared and flickered, and the weight of every unanswered question hung like the heavy clouds cast above the horizon.

It was here, at this crossroads of reality and illusion, that he pondered the very fabric of understanding. The equations scribbled in Horn's notes flickered in his mind like fireflies in the dark, hinting at connection points within the labyrinth of life, yet each connection felt woefully incomplete. Standing so close to the surface, he felt the magnetic pull of truths that eluded him, mysteries hovering just beyond the edge of comprehension. What lay beyond the rationality of his translations, beyond the established borders of logic and intellect?

In the dim light, he recalled Selma's riddle-like warnings: "Some maps chart territories from which one cannot return." The very essence of knowledge had become an enticing yet perilous game. Would he dare to follow his instincts further into the depths? The convergence Horn had alluded to was not merely a merging of celestial bodies but a synthesis of the tangible and the spectral. He envisioned a reality where possibilities spiralled infinitely and where he could dissolve the barriers of his ordinary, measured life.

With every passing moment, however, a gnawing unease began to burgeon within him. As he leaned closer to the lake, an otherworldly chill crawled along his spine. Was he prepared to confront the abyss he sensed lurking in the water? Would crossing the threshold of knowledge lead to enlightenment or madness? Karim shuddered at the thought, feeling as though a part of him teetered on the brink of both a profound revelation and an unbearable void.

The reflections on the lake danced mockingly, now resembling ancient forms that hinted of lost secrets and undefined paths through time. As the wind howled in his ear, Karim understood that he was standing at the precipice of a decision that could unravel his very existence. Curiosity or fear; knowledge or the unknown?

With breath held in anticipation, the hum of the world around him grew louder, and the threshold beckoned him forward into the uncharted chaos that lay just beyond.

As Karim stood at the edge of the Lake of Tunis, the waters shimmered with the wavering light of the setting sun, casting a golden hue that blurred the line between earth and sky. The lake mirrored his internal turmoil; just as the surface transitioned from solidity to fluidity, so too did his grasp on reality become less certain. Waves lapped against the shore in an echo of whispers long forgotten, tales spun within the labyrinthine alleys of the Medina, tales he had begun to question, as shadows danced on the periphery of his vision.

He remembered Selma's words, spoken in that ethereal cadence of hers, 'What you perceive, my dear, sometimes lies in the folds of an illusion. Truth is often as slippery as the waters before you.' It was a riddle that gnawed at his thoughts, making him wonder about the fine veil separating wisdom from delusion. Each corner he turned in the Medina felt like a flickering flame in the dark, illuminating fragments of knowledge while casting deeper shadows that threatened to engulf him.

The convergence of thoughts cascaded like the currents beneath the lake's surface, churning with mounting anxiety. He had spent countless nights piecing together Horn's scattered notes, only to realise that some truths may forever evade him. Did he truly seek knowledge, or was he merely chasing phantoms of insight, each revelation leading him deeper into an illusion of understanding? The question lingered in the air, thick with tension. He scanned the horizon, where the sun dipped lower, questioning whether he was gazing at a truth painted in the vivid colours of twilight or if it was merely a mirage, dissolving as he reached for it.

With each breath, the waters of the lake seemed to whisper of the past and the unseen. They echoed secrets of Horn's disappearance, entangling Karim in a web of paranoia and curiosity. Suddenly, the light dimmed as the clouds gathered, forming a heavy shroud over the once-vibrant scene. Goosebumps prickled his skin, and as the first raindrops fell, they seemed to ignite the air, sharpening his senses. Was this the convergence foretold in Horn's notes? The weather had shifted, and so had the atmosphere, thick with the promise of revelation or frightful ambiguity.

He could not help but remember how the city had shifted around him. An ever-changing labyrinth that reflected his own internal chaos. Each alley he had traversed felt like a living being, pulsating with stories and secrets, bending time and distorting perceptions. He had become a cartographer of this new reality, tracing paths that might lead him to knowledge or madness. He felt both the thrill of discovery and the weight of impending doom pressing upon him.

As the rain intensified, a strange figure appeared on the other side of the lake. Dark and blurred, standing against the deluge, almost as if summoned from the very depths of the illusions he had been grappling with. Heart racing, he tried to discern the form, feeling the familiar tendrils of both fear and fascination wrapping around his heart. Was it a lingering remnant of Horn, or an embodiment of the knowledge Karim sought? The dance between reality and illusion hung heavily in the air, the moment stretched taut as he prepared to step forward into the unknown.

***

14
The Fate of the Cartographer

The burden of Dr. Horn's legacy weighed heavily on Karim as he sat in his small flat, surrounded by strewn notes and incomplete diagrams. The air felt thick with questions, and the stagnant silence echoed the uncertainties swirling within him. Had Horn, the enigmatic cartographer, truly charted a course toward enlightenment, or had he veered into the maddening maelstrom of obsession? This reckoning loomed like a shadow over Karim's own quest.

In his mind, Horn was not just a historical figure; he was a reflection of Karim's own passions and potential follies. Each scribbled note took Karim deeper into the labyrinth of knowledge, making him wonder if Horn had discovered a truth beyond mere understanding. Each time he retraced the Anemoi Map, a mix of excitement and fear coursed through him: what if this pursuit revealed not truths, but more layers of enigma?

Suddenly, a shiver ran down his spine as he recalled Selma's riddles. "Some maps chart territories from which one cannot return," she had warned, her voice echoing in his mind. Was he nearing a similar precipice? Each location he visited resonated uncomfortably with a sense of inevitability; the scent of jasmine that filled the air in the Medina, the whispers that danced between the shadows, all grew more vivid, more urgent. What awaited him in La Marsa on the night of the convergence? Would the merest glimpse of the truth reveal enlightenment or plunge him into chaos?

The once-clear line between the ordinary and the extraordinary began to blur, suggesting that Horn's disappearance might have stemmed from the very knowledge he sought to unveil. Like tendrils of smoke, the memory of Horn's passion intertwined with threads of madness, making the question agonisingly personal for Karim. The maps he was constructing were not merely theoretical. They became alive with possibility, drenched in the palpable pulse of the city's breath.

Knees weak and heart racing, he glanced at the clock. Time had slipped through his fingers, and the convergence loomed closer, yet the answers remained elusive. Karim realised his choice was no longer merely academic; it had morphed into a personal journey, one where success or failure held consequences far greater than he could initially comprehend. The shadow of madness cast by Horn began to envelop him, binding him to an insatiable thirst for discovery. Would he find clarity in the depths, or would he be swallowed whole by the labyrinthine mysteries of the Medina?

As he prepared to finalise his Anemoi Map, he felt it. The undeniable weight of Horn's legacy, both a beacon and a warning. The call of the unknown surged through him, demanding that he step forward into the twisting alleys where past and present converged. The answer to whether Horn had succeeded or failed beckoned him closer, and with it came the truth that perhaps, in the pursuit of knowledge, both outcomes resided side by side, waiting to be uncovered.

As the sun dipped below the horizon, the Medina transformed, shadows elongating and intertwining like whispered secrets in the fading light. Karim wandered through the narrow streets, his senses heightened, acutely aware of a presence that felt both familiar and distant. Horn's theories flickered in his mind, intertwining with the fabric of the city itself, as if the very stones beneath his feet held ancient echoes of the past.

The scent of jasmine mingled with the spicy warmth of the souk, each inhalation bringing memories simmering to the surface. When he paused, he could almost hear fleeting voices, remnants of conversations from long ago, calling out to him through the layers of time.

They rose and fell like the tide, leaving traces of wisdom intertwined with longing. He recalled Selma's riddles about listening to the city's breath, and he focused, trying to disentangle the threads within the chaotic tapestry surrounding him.

As night fell, Karim approached the fountain described in Horn's notes, an unremarkable spot cloaked in shadows. It bubbled softly, each droplet glimmering like a teardrop from another era. He leaned closer, his heart racing. Here, he had been assured by Horn's fragmented words, was a nexus where metaphysical winds might converge. He could feel it. A potent energy gathering in the cool air. It enveloped him, beckoning him to delve deeper into the mystery that had consumed his thoughts.

With every shred of clarity, doubt crept in. Was he losing himself in this pursuit, overwhelmed by fragmented maps and phantom memories? He looked around, half-expecting to see Horn himself appear amid the shadows, a ghostly cartographer guiding him through the birthright of forgotten stories. Silently, he weighed his choices, balancing the possibility of revelation against the haunting idea of madness that lurked just beyond his grasp.

And then, just as uncertainty threatened to extinguish the flickering flame of hope within him, he glimpsed movement in his peripheral vision. Karim turned sharply. There, at the edge of the fountain's glow, stood a figure. Translucent, almost shimmering. It was a woman, her attire reminiscent of ancient times, her face obscured yet strangely familiar. As she stepped forward, the night air shifted, carrying the scent of salt and jasmine together, an enticement and a warning.

"You seek the map that threads through time," she spoke, her voice a melodic whisper, barely rising above the cadence of falling water. "But beware, for every path drawn leads not only to knowledge but also to a choice. A choice that can unravel the very fabric of your being."

The city pulsed around him, alive with shadows that seemed to ripple in agreement. The weight of her words settled into his bones as he struggled to decipher their meaning. Was this a warning or an invitation? Suddenly, the air seemed heavier, thick with the electricity of possibility and peril. He stood frozen, paranoia creeping into the edges of his consciousness. What if Horn was not merely lost, but had traversed beyond, into realms better left unexplored?

"You must decide, Karim," she urged, stepping closer. "Will you follow the whispers that guide you, or will you heed the silence that speaks of caution?"

As her gaze locked onto his, the night deepened, the shadows danced around them like a haunting lullaby, echoing the turmoil brewing within his heart. The echoes of the Medina swirled like an intoxicating fog, each breath daring him to surrender entirely to the map or to the dark abyss that awaited just beyond.

***

As Karim wandered through the Medina, his thoughts were a whirlwind of conflicting emotions. The legacy of knowledge was a double-edged sword; on one hand, it offered pathways into the soul of the city, while on the other, it bore the weight of ensnaring understanding. Would Horn's journey into the heart of this legacy lead to enlightenment or despair? The haunting echoes of the past whispered through the narrow alleys, weaving themselves into the fabric of his thoughts.

The intoxicating blend of spices and jasmine filled the air as he made his way towards a secluded courtyard. Here, hidden beneath the shadows of ancient stone, he had often found solace. A place where he could sit and reflect, scribbling notes and thoughts as they unfurled in his mind. Today, however, the atmosphere felt different, pregnant with anticipation. It was as if the very stones beneath him vibrated with the murmurs of those who had come before, their wisdom lingering like the scent of the sea mingling with the dust of history.

Karim's own sense of insignificance began to grip him. He recalled Horn's ambitious theories about the Anemoi Mapping and its implication that the city's true essence could be charted in the hues of time and memory. But as he unrolled the tattered remnants of Horn's notes, he was confronted with a gnawing fear: Was he merely documenting layers of illusion, or was he poised on the brink of deciphering a profound truth? This thought clung to him as he traced his fingers over the faded ink, each line a reminder of Horn's disappearance. A testament to the potential perils that accompanied the relentless quest for knowledge.

With each passing moment, the atmosphere thickened, and Karachi felt the weight of the decision that lay ahead. Should he forge onward, summing up his findings into a coherent theory, or dismantle the construct he had so painstakingly pieced together? A shadow fell across the courtyard, pulling him from his reverie. For a fleeting moment, Karim caught a glimpse of a figure in the distance, shrouded in the fabric of twilight. The apparition bore an uncanny resemblance to Horn, an ethereal echo of the cartographer who had wandered these streets long before him.

His heart raced, and a sense of urgency filled the air. Karim stood poised between the past and the present, feeling the pulse of the city quicken around him. The fragrance of jasmine thickened, intertwining with the scent of freshly ground spices, drawing him deeper into the labyrinth of the Medina. Could he allow himself to plunge into this metaphysical dance, to explore the echoes that called from other realms, or would he succumb to the madness that Horn had risked?

As night began to cloak the streets, shadows lengthened and whispered, "Choose."

That single word reverberated within him, an invitation laced with foreboding. The legacy of knowledge was not just a pursuit; it was a haunting, a reminder of the enigmatic layers that concealed the truths they both sought. The paths forged from their choices would intertwine, shaping destinies in ways unseen, like the mercurial winds that carried ephemeral echoes through the very soul of Tunis. Karim could feel his grasp on reality slipping as he stood before the threshold of revelation, the weight of Horn's legacy resting heavily upon him.

15
The Breath of the City

While the sun was going down and casting an amber light over the maze-like paths of the Medina, Karim stood on the edge of Lake Tunis, exhausted and aware. The city was alive, its breath a rhythm of distant conversations, the whisper of the Sirocco weaving through the alleyways, mingling with the scent of jasmine and spice. It was at this moment, suspended between possibility and the weight of knowledge, that Karim felt the pulse of his own resolutions taking shape. He could no longer retreat into solitude, translating forgotten verses while the world outside continued to spin, vibrant and untamed.

His encounters with Selma bin Hazm, whose riddles were wrapped in wisdom, echoed in his mind. Listen to the city's breath, she had urged, her voice a gentle insistence, pressing him to explore the spaces between knowledge and oblivion. The realisation washed over him like a wave: he was no longer merely a translator of poetry, but a potential cartographer of the unseen currents that governed his existence, a role he had assumed through the creation of the Anemoi Map. What if, like Horn, he could navigate the deeper layers of reality, using the Anemoi Mapping as a guide? But the cost loomed over him, a spectre whispering of choices made and paths foregone.

As he traced his fingers over the wrinkled edges of Horn's notes, he felt a surge of apprehension alongside exhilaration. Each line pulsated with the promise of discovery, yet the darker implications of his obsession began to manifest. What if the convergence Horn had described was not merely a cosmic alignment but a temporal fracture? What if it altered not only perception, but existence itself? Karim's heart raced at the thought, caught in a whirlwind of desire and fear. With every breath, he sensed that the boundaries between clarity and madness were not merely paper-thin; they were ephemeral shadows, shifting with each gust of wind.

The evening air thickened, as if charged with anticipation. Karim's mind raced back to the fragmented moments that had led him here: the scent of the souks, the echoes of distant voices, the ghostly figures flitting through the Medina. Each experience was a thread in the intricate tapestry of what he could become. And yet, the spectre of Horn haunted him. Had the esteemed scholar uncovered truths too profound to bear? Or had the knowledge he sought driven him to an abyss from which there was no return?

As twilight embraced the city, casting shadows that danced ominously across the ancient walls, Karim felt a shudder ripple through the ground beneath his feet. The city's breath quickening, urging him to make a choice. Would he complete his Anemoi Map, risking his very essence in pursuit of an unfathomable truth? Or would he withdraw, encasing himself in the safety of routine, forever haunted by the question of what might have been? The weight of the decision pressed heavily upon him, converging with the pulse of the city, drawing him closer to the precipice of his resolution.

This was not merely a choice of knowledge; it was a reckoning with the very nature of existence. Karim inhaled deeply, letting the warmth of the city fill his lungs. At that moment, he understood. Perhaps it was not the destination that mattered, but the act of courage in embracing both clarity and ambiguity. With that revelation, Karim stepped forward, ready to confront whatever the tides of the uncharted might unveil.

With the evening sun casting long shadows over the Medina, Karim stood at the threshold of the hidden alley he had meticulously mapped, his heart racing as he recalled the whispered words of Selma bin Hazm. The city breathes, each alley, each stone a part of its soul, she had said, urging him to listen closely. But as he stared into the dim recesses of the dimly lit path, uncertainty tangled with his anticipation. The air held an electric tension, pregnant with possibilities waiting to unfurl.

His fingers brushed against the worn edges of the 'Anemoi Map' he'd crafted. A living testament to his journey through intertwined memories and shifting realities, each fragment a piece of the past that shaped his present. Each line and curve bore the weight of intentions that once pulsed with clarity, yet now seemed to beckon him towards an unfurling tapestry of uncertainty. He thought of Dr. Horn, the enigmatic figure whose fate remained a haunting question mark. The realisation dawned that his pursuit for clarity might instead lead him deeper into the tangible embrace of the unknown.

As he stepped forward, the atmosphere thickened, swirling with the scents of spices mixed with the lingering essence of jasmine. Karim felt the city shift around him, suggesting that these unwritten possibilities were not mere figments of a vivid imagination, but tangible threads woven through the city's very fabric. Echoes of conversations floated through the air. Serendipitous phrases from poems he'd translated, full of longing and whispers of wisdom, both beckoning and disorienting. Each step he took echoed, not just against the stones, but through the folds of time itself.

In the labyrinthine embrace of the Medina, Karim sensed that all the wisdom he had so ardently pursued was entangled with the reckless abandon of the unwritten. Visions of the future danced before him like flickering candle flames. Seeds of potential languished, waiting for the breeze of his choices to breathe life into them. The city's breath, intertwined with his own, was urging him forward, sharpening his senses to the delicate balance between risk and revelation.

Yet, lurking behind the allure of discovery was the spectre of consequence. Karim paused, the weight of choices pressing down. What would happen if he strayed too far into this elusive path? Could he find a way back, or was the abyss of the city ready to cradle him into its enigmatic depths? Doubts wove into his mind like strands of silk. Each longing to ensnare him, pulling him into an uncertainty rich with danger and beauty.

He knew he stood at the brink of something transformative; fuelled by curiosity, he realised the unwritten possibilities were not merely future paths yet untravelled but the manifest potential of every moment. The chance to embody change and beckon understanding from the currents of existence itself. Each inhalation filled him with resolve as he walked further into the heart of the city, propelled by the intoxicating promise of unravelling his destiny amid the layers of Tunisia's storied past.

As Karim rounded a corner, the air stilled, and the alley opened into a small courtyard where the city seemed to sigh heavily, enveloped in an air of waiting. He felt it. A throbbing pulse beneath his feet, as if the very ground beneath him was a vessel of unwritten tales longing to be told. Silhouettes flitted at the edges of his vision, figures draped in the winding fabric of history, weaving through the spaces he could sense but not fully perceive. At that moment, the breath of the city became a thunderous dirge of possibilities, unveiling a haunting truth: to seek knowledge often demands more than mere understanding; it necessitates a surrendering to the unfolding chaos of life itself.

With heart pounding in cadence with the city's breath, Karim took a step forward. Into the thrilling, terrifying embrace of the unwritten possibilities that lay before him, aware now that every choice he made could fracture reality or illuminate the shadows, offering him a glimpse of the deeper truths locked within the labyrinth of existence.

***

As Karim stood at the water's edge, the Lake of Tunis shimmered beneath the waning moonlight, a restless canvas reflecting a cosmos both familiar and eerily alien. He could feel the weight of the moment pressing down on him, a culmination of all he had experienced in the twisting alleys of the Medina and the cryptic wisdom imparted by Selma. Every whispering breeze, every uncertain echo conjured fragments of Horn's notes, memories interwoven with the scents of jasmine and distant sea salt.

The dusk huddled around him like a shroud, cradling ambiguities that thrummed with life. He closed his eyes, recalling the instructions embedded in those frayed papers. How to harness the metaphysical winds, to listen to the city's breath as it inhaled possibilities and exhaled shadows. Yet, the more he understood, the more the lines between reality and illusion blurred, revealing layers of existence that felt as precarious as shifting sand.

During that instant, his desire for resolution was in direct opposition to the disorder of his thoughts. Should he trust in the wisdom of the winds or surrender to the fear of what lay beyond? Was enlightenment waiting at the cusp of his choices, or madness lurking in the intricate folds of the unknown? The wind howled, a cacophony of voices interspersed with fleeting laughter, the sound of his own heart racing against the fears mirrored in the lake's depths.

Dizzy with uncertainty, Karim opened his eyes to the moonlit expanse, the water echoing his internal tempest. The convergence was almost upon him. A rare alignment of cosmic forces that Horn had seemed to believe held the key to unveiling truths veiled beyond mere understanding. Here, he was merely a cartographer attempting to navigate the unfathomable, to glean a map of existence from the stars and shadows pressing in around him.

Driven by desperation, he turned back toward the Medina, its labyrinthine paths twisting like thoughts caught in a web of indecision. Each alley beckoned with a promise of revelation, each corner held the echo of the past, yet he sensed a growing unease that warned him. There would be no easy answers, only the haunting spectre of ambiguity looming over him. And yet, he had ventured too far and too deeply to turn back now; he was entwined in the fate of the city.

With each step, his determination solidified, compelled forward by an invisible thread woven through the fabric of the city, leading him to a revelation of sorts. Shadows flitted among the stalls, voices entwined in a magnetic dance of stories both consumed and forgotten. Nevertheless, despite the chaos, he sensed an underlying order. A pull guiding him to the heart of his own existence, the exquisite, bittersweet nature of what it meant to seek.

As he embraced the ambiguity of it all, Karim felt a surge of clarity wash over him. Perhaps the essence of existence lay not in the finality of answers, but rather in the beauty of the questions themselves. A meandering path through clarity and perplexity, entangled. With that thought, he resolved to plunge deeper into the embrace of the city, ready to confront the unanswered. The hidden labyrinths waiting to be explored, and the elusive answers veiled within the ambiguity of existence itself.